Carl Weber Presents:

Ride or Die Chick 4

Carl Weber Presents:

Ride or Die Chick 4

by

J.M. Benjamin

Dedication

To my number 1 rider, my mother, Rev. Jean M. Word,
and to all those who have been riding for me thus far.
Thank You!
-J.M.

Prologue

"Naked I came from my mother's womb and naked I will depart. The Lord giveth and the Lord has taketh away. May the name of the Lord be praised. Ashes to ashes and dust to dust," the Irish priest pronounced as he sprinkled dust on top of the casket. Everyone began tossing red roses onto Sammy Black Sr.'s casket.

"May God be with you and the family," was what Sammy Black Jr. had been hearing all day long followed by countless kisses and hugs. He stood and watched as they lowered his father in the ground of their Ireland homeland. He tossed a handful of dirt onto Sammy Black Sr.'s coffin.

"Until we meet again, ol' chum," he whispered under his breath.

He lowered his shades to shield his misty eyes, then did an about face and made his way toward his car. He nodded, shook hands, embraced hugs, and kissed cheeks until he reached his Lincoln luxury sedan, where his driver waited.

"You okay, sir?" his driver asked in a solemn tone.

No, I am not okay, he wanted to say. Instead he nodded, then climbed into his Lincoln. *But I will be,* he continued with his thought, as he peered out of the backseat window.

The ol' man would be proud, he thought as he watched the sea of people, who had come to pay their respects, make their way to their vehicles. The first part of his obligation was done. He had carried out his father's wishes about the way he wanted to be laid to rest. It wasn't a surprise to him that his father had left specific instructions in his will to be buried next to his parents. They were buried on the land that had been in their family for generations. It had cost a lot of money and footwork to pull it off, but there was no amount of money or headache that would prevent Sammy Black Jr. from carrying out his father's requests. The environmental health inspector from the local authority's health department gave him a hard time about making sure the burial site didn't pollute any water sources or drainage channels. The depth of the holes had to be eight feet. Then there were the crooked politicians who saw an opportunity to obtain funding for future campaigns, whose palms he had to grease to ensure all paperwork was approved fast enough to bury his father on private grounds. The cost of the burial itself and getting the preparations finished, from invites to all other funeral amenities, alone was enough to stress him out. But he knew he had to keep a level head and not let anyone see him sweat. In all, Sammy Jr. kicked out over one hundred grand to send his father home respectfully.

The money was the least of his worries and concern. He told himself that this was one of the things his father had groomed him for. He had been receiving calls from all of the tops of the other families offering their condolences about his loss. He knew their main concern was the financial loss they were all taking because of the situation. Sammy Jr. was not in the least bit surprised by the calls and the extent of the conversation. He was also not surprised when a meeting was called. He didn't know what to expect at the meeting, which was why he had all of his men on high alert and ready for whatever. He was not sure whether the death of his father was an inside job.

Although he hadn't fully gotten all the particulars, according to their contacts in law enforcement a young black couple randomly ran up in their storefront stash house and lucked out. He found the story hard to believe. He was under a lot of pressure and knew he had to get to the bottom of the situation as soon as possible. He had already told himself that if it came out that one of the families had anything to do with the death of his father he was all too prepared to go to war to defend their family's honor.

He was somewhat relieved when he found out that the meeting he was invited to was called to announce him as the new boss of his family. Still, the entire time he searched faces and questioned handshakes and hugs. His father had always told him, "Every smile is not a pleasant one and not every handshake is attached to respect." It wasn't until now that he realized the depth of his father's words.

It was no secret; he had been prepped to become the head of the family in the event something were to happen to his father. Both his father and grandfather once ruled with an iron fist for nearly two decades. Now, after his father's untimely demise, Sammy Black Jr. realized it was his turn. Not only had he become the top dog overnight, as the boss, he had also inherited the responsibility of retrieving what was taken from the family during his father's death. He knew it wasn't personal, just business. The merchandise was taken on his father's watch, which made that Sammy Jr.'s problem. He was certain that's why the meeting to make him head of his family was put in motion so quickly. They wanted him to start tracking down what was taken from them. He knew his new position and how long he held it in the organization depended on whether he got back what belonged to them and took care of those responsible.

He ran his hand from the top of his red buzz cut down to his face, shook his head, and grimaced. In his mind, no matter how long it took, he would track down those responsible for the slaying of his father. And when he did, he would carry out the second part of his obligation to his family and his father.

Chapter One

Fifty-two-year-old Robert Cole cruised through the downtown area of Richmond, Virginia, in search of potential customers in need of his services. He had been a taxi driver for the last fifteen years of his existence and couldn't recall having had a worse day. Not only did he have a migraine headache that had been relentlessly pounding away at his skull for the past eight hours, but business had been slow all week. On top of that, the air conditioner in his taxi had been broken for just as long, so he had been riding around with the windows down, sweating profusely from the sweltering Virginia heat. Only the fact that the sun had gone down some and night began to fall made it better, but not much. Normally he wouldn't be working in the particular area, but tonight he was desperate, and desperate times called for desperate measures. He was flat broke with no food in the house. He could literally hear his stomach whining as he drove in search of potential customers. Had it not been for the fact that he had gone nearly three days without eating already and his taxi's gas light had been on for just as long, he would have turned back around and called it a night.

"Jesus H. Christ!" Robert Cole swore as he wiped his brow with the handkerchief he had clenched in his right hand.

He didn't swear because of the heat though. He had used the Lord's name in vain out of disappointment.

Judging by the caliber of people roaming the downtown streets, he began to think it was a bad idea choosing to try his luck. In his eyes, all of the black faces he rode past were up to no good. His belief came from the bad experience he had endured a few years back.

He was the victim of an attempted robbery in Richmond not too far from where he was traveling now. Ultimately, he walked away scot-free but a young black teen was left dead. Let him tell it, had it not been for the licensed .38 revolver he possessed, he would have been shot and killed instead, despite the fact that no weapon belonging to the teen was found. Although he had been cleared of all charges and the incident was ruled as self-defense, the incident still haunted him. He had been shaken up ever since. He tried to steer clear of that part of town out of fear of possibly being recognized by one of the young black teen's angry loved ones. But the hunger pains in his stomach overrode that fear. He was all too prepared and wouldn't hesitate to use the .25 pearl-handle, nickel-plated semiautomatic pistol he now toted under his driver seat, if he had to. He refused to be the victim again, especially at the hands of some young black street punk.

Truth be told, Robert had a special kind of hatred for blacks since his run-in with the young teen. He found himself becoming a racist, often referring to people of color as African Americans in public, but in privacy he used the word "nigger" to best describe or refer to blacks. That was when he was in a good mood.

The altercation that had happened wasn't the first time he'd had an incident with a black person. He actually bumped heads with blacks quite often. Whenever he saw a black person he expected trouble. He'd been written up several times and even suspended once. Because he had so many years on the job and was a part of the union, they couldn't flat-out fire him.

Although he despised young black males, he was actually secretly fond of young black girls with tight bodies, which was why he came to a screeching halt when he saw the extended arm attached to the beautiful caramel specimen on the opposite side of the road. Robert put on his left blinker and made a U-turn in the middle of the street. Abruptly stopping in front of the pretty girl, he rolled down his passenger window.

"Need a ride, sweetie?" Robert Cole flashed his coffee-stained teeth.

"Yes, can you help me? I'm lost." She flashed him a warm smile.

"Sure, where you headed?"

"I need to get to Chamberlain and Lombardy."

"Aw, that's not that far. For you, that'll be seven dollars," Robert Cole informed the girl. He could already taste the triple-decker cheeseburger from the twenty-four-hour Wendy's. His mouth watered at the thought. "Hop on in!"

He peered up at the young, pretty girl. He could see the nervous look on her face. "Is there something wrong, sweetheart?" he asked. He had his suspicion about her facial expression, but needed to be sure.

"I . . . I . . ." the girl stammered. "I don't have seven dollars." She dropped her head in shame.

Her words went straight to the pit of Robert Cole's stomach. His original hunger pains resurfaced and mixed with a new set of hunger pains from getting his hopes up too high. *Shit! Fuckin' black cunt,* he cursed the girl out in his mind. He took another look up at her. His mind began to travel somewhere else: right between his legs. Lust invaded his thoughts. *I haven't made any money practically all day; the least I can do is treat myself and have a little fun before I clock out,* he reasoned with himself.

"It's okay. I'm sure we can work something out," Robert Cole offered.

His words caused the girl to raise her head. She nodded innocently.

Robert Cole hit the locks to the back door of the taxi. His circumcised penis began to stiffen as he peered in the rearview mirror into the back seat of the taxi. His eyes zeroed in on the young girl's thick caramel thighs. He dropped his hand in his lap and brushed it across his hardness as he stared at them protruding out of the jean shorts that rode all the way up in between her legs. His eyes trailed up until he could see her face. His heart nearly stopped as she licked her luscious lips in an inconspicuous manner. His imagination ran wild at the thought of her mouth on him. He threw the taxi out of park. Within seconds, he was cruising up the street.

She's going to suck this cock and love it, thought Robert as he searched for a secluded area. Moments later, he made a right onto a side street that appeared pitch black from a distance. He pulled over, put the taxi in park, and killed his lights.

"Get out and come on up here, sugar." Robert Cole unlocked the doors.

He began unbuckling his belt in a speedy manner as the caramel girl exited the back of the taxi. He was so anxious he fumbled with unbuttoning his pants. Just as he got the button to open, the driver's door of the taxi flew open. When he peered up he was met with a pistol to the upper side of his face. Robert Cole's dick instantly shriveled up at the sight of the caramel girl, who he thought would be sucking his dick, standing in front of him brandishing a pistol.

"Son of a bitch!" he cursed. He couldn't believe his dumb luck.

His left eye was burning due to the blood dripping from the side of his head. With the eye he could see with, there was no mistaking the murderous look he saw in the caramel girl's eyes. His entire life flashed before his eyes right before the explosion. Urine began to trickle down the inner part of his pants legs, soiling his light blue denim Wrangler jeans. The thought of possibly dying over greed and lust ran through his mind. The blow caught him off guard and knocked him off balance. Blood gushed out of the side of his forehead and leaked into his left eye, but the first shot didn't kill him. It had entered and exited the side of his face. Before he had time to react and try to reach for his own weapon, he was hit again. The second tore into the right side of his neck. Blood sprayed the inside of the taxi's front driver's side window. Robert Cole let out one of the loudest screams he had ever let out in his life.

"What the . . ." was all that escaped his lips before she grabbed him up by the collar and yanked him out of the taxi.

"Get out, you perverted piece of shit!" Baby barked.

Robert Cole grabbed hold of his pants as he plunged to the ground. He stared up and saw the barrel of Baby's gun aimed directly at him. A confused look was plastered all over his face. At that moment, he knew he should have gone with his first instinct about working the black-infested area.

"I should shoot your fucking little white dick off!" Baby growled. She lowered the gun and jerked it in Robert Cole's direction, between his legs, to put emphasis on her statement.

"Get your bitch ass up!" she commanded.

Robert Cole did as he was told. He fastened his jeans then nervously stood up. He was scared for his life. The look on Baby's face was psychotic. It was like she had an unquenchable thirst for hurting him. He was so frightened that he nearly lost control of his bowels. His stomach began to twist in knots. But it was not a notification of how hungry he was. His hunger pains had been replaced and turned into a warning sign for the danger he knew he was in. Bad enough he had just pissed himself. Now, here it was: he stood there in fear, clenching his ass cheeks as he struggled to buckle his belt while fighting to keep from shitting on himself. The distorted look he made while trying to prevent that from happening seemed to please Baby. Gas escaped the crease of his squeezed cheeks. The smell lingered in the air and found its way toward Baby's nostrils. She covered her nose.

"Nasty-ass cracker," she spat. "Give me your fucking wallet," she chimed.

"I don't have a dime," Robert Cole warned her as he reached for his wallet. *I wish my gun were behind my back instead of in the car because you'd be one dead black bitch.*

He tossed Baby his wallet. She bent down and picked it up, the whole time never taking her eyes off of Robert Cole. She opened it up and scanned it. "I need this taxi, Mr. Robert L. Cole, 1964 . . ." She began to read off his address to him.

Robert Cole immediately got the picture. "I understand." He nodded. "Take it."

"I'll leave it unharmed once I get another ride. Lucky for you, I'm not going to kill you. Your day will come though, you piece of shit."

A sigh of relief swept through Robert Cole's body. He had been sure Baby was going to leave him for dead.

"Where's your cell phone?" Baby asked.

Robert Cole cursed under his breath. He was hoping she'd leave without checking. He knew it was in his best interest not to play with her. He pulled his old-model flip phone out of his front pocket and tossed it over to Baby.

Baby picked it up and tucked it in her shirt. She back-pedaled her way to the taxi then hopped in. "Turn over and lie on your fat stomach, you piece of shit, and count to a thousand," Baby instructed him.

Robert Cole did as he was told. She kicked him in his ass, causing him to let out a grunt.

"A thousand motherfuka'!" She repeated.

Seconds later, Baby was headed to where she had left Treacherous tucked away in the car. She knew it was just a matter of time before the police tracked down the car they had fled. She couldn't afford any mishaps. Not when the love of her life's own life was on the line.

She was focused. Her only thought now was getting Treacherous some medical attention. Baby pulled up to where she had parked the stolen car. She looked over at Treacherous. He was still unconscious. She took hold of his wrist. She became somewhat relieved once she felt a pulse, but she knew she was running out of time. Baby struggled to load two large, heavy duffle bags into the trunk of the taxi. She then transferred Treacherous from one vehicle to the other. Moments later, she peeled off in the stolen taxi.

Chapter Two

You killed my mother. I won't ever forget you! were the words that echoed in Andre Randle's mind as he struggled to find a comfortable position to lay in. The discomfort from his injuries to the shoulder and face kept him up tossing and turning for most of the night. It had been the norm for the past few evenings after his release from the hospital. The painkillers he had been prescribed by the physician didn't do anything to ease the pain. Instead, the pills had caused him to become nauseous, overly sensitive, and emotional so he discontinued taking them. He chose to fight the pain off naturally and was now realizing how difficult it actually was.

He couldn't help but reflect on why he was laid up in bed in the first place. Ever since the gun battle at Detective Love's house, his first encounter with Treacherous Freeman Jr. kept playing in his mind. The words, *"You killed my mother,"* repeated over and over in Andre Randle's head. *Yeah, kid, I had to, or else she was going to put a bullet in your skull,* he wanted to say back to young Treacherous that day; but he knew it was not the right or appropriate thing to say. Now, here it was: a young and dangerous man with a vendetta toward him was roaming the streets of Virginia. That didn't sit well with Andre Randle.

He remembered how he tried his best to defuse the situation. *"Hold your fire!"* he yelled out to *Teflon Jackson.*

Andre Randle sat upright. He reached over and grabbed the pack of Newport 100s on his nightstand. The nicotine from the cigarette seemed to relax him. Andre Randle closed his eyes and let out a gust of silver smoke. He shook his head as his pleading words replayed themselves in the front of his head: *"Ms. Jackson, please don't do this, and don't do this to your child!"* he remembered saying to her.

"Fuck that! It's not my fault!" he bellowed. "I did all I could. She made a choice." He continued to talk aloud to himself. An image of Teflon putting the gun to young Treacherous's head illuminated in Andre Randle's mind right before he heard the loud boom and saw the flashing white light.

Andre Randle's eyes shot open. He shook the image of Teflon Jackson's suicide by cop out of his head and turned on the television to get his mind off of his present condition. He rubbed the swollen part of his face gently while he flicked through channel after channel with nothing in particular in mind to watch. He surfed through cartoons, reality shows, and reruns of *CSI*. He shook his head at the fact that nothing on television seemed to interest him, not even the news, and that was his favorite thing to watch. Today he was just not in the mood for anything. He was simply going through the motions. No matter how much he tried, he just couldn't shake the thought of what happened back at Arthur Love's house between the two of them, Love's daughter, and Treacherous Freeman. It was a close call, but they had survived. His only regret was that he and Love were unable to finish what they had started together, which was take down the Bonnie and Clyde couple.

He stopped pressing the channel button on the remote when he came across the Discovery channel. He was sure that if anything could relax his mind, it would be watching something dealing with nature. Just as he was about to get into the show featured, his mind did a quick backtrack. Subconsciously he thought he had recognized something or, rather, someone a few channels back. Randle's television slowly traveled backward as he pointed the remote at the screen. Four stations later, he could not believe his eyes. He increased the volume on the television as his mouth fell open at the photo on the television screen.

"Authorities still have no leads as to the whereabouts of the suspects in connection to the murder of alleged Irish crime boss Samuel Duff, known as Sammy Black. Mr. Black was buried in his homeland of Ireland some days ago. We'll have more as this story continues to unfold."

"Christ," Andre Randle cursed as he switched to another channel. He had no luck finding the report on any other station. Normally he would have been watching the news, but since being out of the hospital and taking the medication he had been prescribed he hadn't been up on anything as of late. For Richmond news to make it all the way over to the seven cities' news meant whoever Treacherous Freeman and Baby Love killed was a major figure in the underworld.

"This just keeps getting better and better." He let out a disheartened chuckle.

He flung the cover off his body with his good arm. *Time to get up,* he told himself as he climbed out of bed. A sharp pain jolted through his shoulder as he rose. He shook it off. He shifted his head from side to side, cracking his neck, then did some basic stretching and leg lifts to get the blood circulating in his body. Andre Randle was beginning to feel rejuvenated. He was ready to get back on the horse and ride out what he and Detective Arthur Love had started. With that in mind, he knew what he had to do when the sun came up.

Chapter Three

Arthur Love bent down and picked up the newspaper that had been delivered and placed on his doorstep. For once the front page didn't headline his fugitive daughter and her boyfriend. He placed the newspaper on the kitchen table then made his way to the fridge and snatched up the carton of eggs and box of Caroline sausage. Minutes later, the smell of pork sausages filled the air as he scrambled three eggs in a bowl. He couldn't help but think about his daughter as he prepared the meal. It was Baby's favorite one to make for him. It was also the last thing she had made. He shook his head as he scrambled the eggs in the small frying pan. He tossed two slices of Kraft white cheese onto the eggs. His mind wandered as he mixed the two. Never would he have imagined that his baby girl would become a wanted woman, running around like a maniac with her thug boyfriend.

"Fuuuuuuck!" he chimed. The impact of his fist slamming down on the kitchen counter nearly knocked it off the hinges. *Where did I go wrong?* he questioned himself for the umpteenth time. He wondered how his once perfect life had turned into what it was today.

So much time had passed. So many unanswered questions and apologies never made, Arthur Love believed, as he thought of how his family had been ripped apart. He had yet to recover from the shocking news Baby had forced her mother to confess to him. And it was still a hard pill to swallow as far as what happened next. He could still hear Baby's cries:

"You were supposed to protect me! You were supposed to protect me! Goddamit!"

Arthur continued fixing his meal in a daze as his mind drifted to visions of his wife's murder at the hands of his daughter, a murder that he knew Baby believed to be warranted and justified. He could hear his wife's words as if it were yesterday.

"I was wrong."

Arthur Love squeezed his eyes tight. He didn't want to relive the ordeal but he could not stop the thoughts that were occupying the space in his mind. Arthur Love watched as he tried to reason with his daughter.

"Baby, I'm begging you. Whatever it is or whatever it was, I'm sorry I wasn't there for you, but I'm here now."

He knew what scene was coming next. He tried to shake it but couldn't. For as long as he lived, Arthur Love would not forget the final moments between him, his wife, and his daughter.

"I hope, wherever you're going, you're forgiven for what you did to me because I never will," were the words Baby said her mother, and, *"Daddy, I'm sorry,"* to him, that echoed in Arthur Love's mind right before his daughter had squeezed the trigger and blown his wife's brains out. He ran his hands down his face. It was as if he could still feel his wife's blood and brain matter on him.

"No!" he cried out.

He felt like a failure as a father. He had let down the two most important people in his life: his wife and daughter. It was the main reason he worked the case so diligently. He knew he couldn't turn back the hands of time; but in his mind he thought if he could at least be the one to get to his daughter first, he could save her life, even if it meant spending the rest of it in prison.

The phone rang, taking Arthur Love away from his thoughts. He looked at the caller ID and grimaced. "Hello."

"Hey, Arthur. I wanted to know if you wanted to meet me at the gym."

"Oh yeah. What time?" Arthur tried to sound interested. He recognized Detective Daniels's voice.

"Can you meet me in an hour?" Detective Daniels asked.

"No. I won't be available until the evening," he declined. Any other time he would have accepted the offer from his colleague and workout partner. Working out was the furthest thing from his mind. He was not in the mood for anything. "Sorry, man. Let me call you later, because someone's at my door," Arthur lied as he ended the call. It wasn't anything personal toward him. It was just the mood he had been in since recuperating. The truth was he had become somewhat of a loner. And today he'd rather indulge in breakfast and not be bothered.

He finished cooking and placed his plate at the table. He thumbed through the newspaper until he located the sports section. His mind drifted again as he read the paper and ate his food. He thought of Baby and the eventful day that changed her life forever. Since that night, he kept asking himself, *was there something that I could have done to prevent the molestation?* No matter what, he still felt somewhat responsible. Baby was a victim of circumstance, he kept telling himself. She was a child and no child deserved to be abused. He felt some type of empathy for his daughter and her actions. Arthur Love somewhat understood why her life had taken the illegal turn that it did. Over many years on the force at Richmond PD he saw many files of sexual abuse, and he had heard it all, from fathers doing bad things to their sons or daughters, or even both in some cases, or parents who made their child perform sexual acts on them; but never did he think it would come to his doorstep.

Arthur Love took the last bite of his meal. He had tried for the last few minutes to take his thoughts away from Baby. He sat at the kitchen table gazing out of the window. He wondered where Baby could be. He didn't know where to begin to possibly find her, but he intended to search high and low, leaving no stone unturned.

Just then, his phone rang, interrupting his thoughts again. When he saw the name flash across the screen, he hoped he didn't have to wonder any longer.

Chapter Four

"You gots to be freakin' kidding me!" Forty-four-year-old Dr. Peter Jackson's eyes shot open. His sleep was broken by the thunderous sound of cages rattling and loud barking on the other side of his bedroom door. He looked over at the alarm clock. It was just a little after two a.m. He flung the warm down comforter off of his body with irritation and climbed out of bed. He was used to being awakened in the middle of the night, all hours of the night for that matter, and was fine with that. He knew it came with the job. But he had just managed to fall asleep nearly an hour ago, after delivering six Labrador retrievers during a C-section, and was not in the mood to be dealing with another cranky animal.

He slipped into his bedroom slippers and sluggishly made his way to his room door. Seconds later, he was feet away from the door to his place of business. Having his workplace intertwined with his residence was like a gift and a curse for Dr. Jackson. This had been the story of his life for the past ten years of being in private practice. He was thankful to the Army for his degree and profession. He was also fortunate to have received an honorable discharge after shattering his pelvis from the impact of a pipe bomb during a terrorist attack in Iraq, versus being shipped home in a body bag. The whole experience left a bad taste in his mouth and deterred him from pursuing the medical field for human life. He didn't believe he had the stomach for it. He still felt obligated to use his God-given talent to help save lives. That's when he came up with the idea of becoming a veterinarian. Since then he had dedicated his life to catering to animals. He came to find that animals could be just as much of a handful as humans when sick or in pain. There were times when he'd have to spend seventy-two hours dealing with an animal under observation. During those long, tiring days, one of the perks was the fact that he didn't have far to travel to get home. But it was times like this, when his patients were riled up or simply being difficult, when he wished the two places were separate.

The closer he got to the door, the louder the barking and cage rattling became. Dr. Jackson shook his head and grimaced as he entered the room.

"Okay! Okay! I'm here!" he announced as he flicked the office light switch on. "What's all the fuss about?" he added as he made his way over to one kennel in particular.

"What's the matter, boy? Huh?" He directed his words to a white spotted terrier, who seemed to be making the most noise out of all the animals. Although he was used to it, he was a little surprised by the terrier's behavior. Since he had found him on the side of Interstate 85 with a broken leg and fractured ribs three weeks ago, just outside of Richmond, all he did was bark and whine the first two weeks. But for the past week he had been pretty quiet like the others. He had been nursing him back to health ever since. He watched as the terrier spun around in circles and continued to let out his high-pitched barks.

A sedative ought to do the trick, thought Dr. Jackson. "Don't worry, I got something for you," he assured the terrier. He stuck his hand through the top of the kennel and massaged behind his left ear. Normally that would do the trick, but the terrier kept barking. He had been so engrossed with the terrier that he hadn't noticed that, aside from the barking dogs, he was not alone.

A sudden voice startled him and caused him to spin around. It all made sense to him. The terrier was not trying to be a peace disturber; he was being a protector and alarm system for Dr. Jackson.

"Who are you?" His words came out choppy. He immediately threw his hands up in the air. His eyes widened at the sight of the gun the intruder was brandishing.

"I'm not here to cause any trouble. This was the only place I could find nearby. We need your help," Baby replied all in one breath.

Dr. Jackson's eyes shifted from Baby to the figure she had laid on his examining table. He could see that both she and who appeared to be an injured male were just young teens. He could only imagine what happened. Lately, he had been hearing about the violence in the Richmond area, from black-on-black crime to police brutality, and he wondered which applied. Whatever the case, being from Glen Allen housing projects himself, he knew how things could easily happen and felt everybody deserved to be helped. The only thing was that it had been a long time since he had attempted to perform any type of medical assistance on another human being. His experience in the medical field since the service was with animals. He couldn't believe the irony of his profession.

"You do know I'm a veterinarian, right?" he stated as a matter of fact.

"Yes. We can't go nowhere else. I'll take my chances," Baby retorted.

Dr. Jackson understood loud and clear. Although animals were his primary clients, he knew there was not much difference with a human life. *What if something goes wrong?* crossed his mind. For his sake, he hoped that would not be the case.

"Okay," he agreed. "But first, I'm going to need you to not point that gun at me. It's making me nervous."

Baby studied him for a second. She then lowered her weapon.

"Thank you." Dr. Jackson made his way over to where Treacherous lay unconscious. He noticed he was sweating profusely. "Now, what happened?"

"My boyfriend's been shot," was all Baby offered.

Dr. Jackson peered over at her. Her stony facial expression was enough to convince him that that was all she was willing to tell him.

"We have to get him out of these bloody clothes," Dr. Jackson informed Baby. He then walked over to the tray table where he kept his medical tools neatly laid out. Baby watched as he twisted the top off of a bottle of peroxide and poured some over the sharp-looking object he held over the small metal pan in his hand. He split Treacherous's shirt open with the sharp blade he'd just retrieved from the tray of tools and sterilized. He noticed the bullet hole in Treacherous's lower chest area oozing blood. Once he had his shirt off completely, he saw a bullet protruding from his forearm.

"Do you know if he's been hit anywhere else?" Dr. Jackson asked Baby.

"I'm not sure."

"Okay." He began cutting Treacherous's pants off of him. Once he'd established there were no other gunshot wounds he sprang into action. He pulled out a pair of rubber surgical gloves and began to selectively pick and choose medical instruments he felt he'd need for what he was about to do. He brought his mask down over his face and placed the instruments in a pan of liquid. Although he always sterilized all of his medical tools, he felt compelled to do it again since he was about to perform on a human being and not an animal.

Once they were all sterilized, he snatched up a bottle of alcohol, iodine, a couple boxes of bandages, and tape.

Every move he made, Baby made. She became his shadow. Dr. Jackson felt smothered, as if he couldn't breathe. Everywhere he turned, she was right there. He asked her to give him some elbow room so that he could operate on Treacherous. Baby nodded and backed up off of him. She went off to the side near the corner of his office. Her pacing back and forth both annoyed and distracted him. Finally, Dr. Jackson got fed up.

He couldn't help but keep looking back over his shoulder at Baby. Realizing she was going to stop, he got fed up.

I'm going to need you to wait out there." He pointed toward his waiting room area.

He knew he wouldn't be able to focus with her in the room hovering all around him.

"I'm not going anywhere," Baby stated.

"Well, then that means you don't care about this young man's life, because it lies in your hands," Dr. Jackson informed her. "It's your call. Wait out there, he lives. Stay in here, he—"

"He dies, you die!" Baby cut Dr. Jackson's words short and finished his sentence for him. Her gun was now pressed up against Dr. Jackson's forehead.

He squeezed his eyes tightly and then opened them. "Young lady, think for a second. Why risk the life of this man, who you apparently love and will ride to the end of the earth for, over something so small? I promise you I will do my best to save this young man's life, but I need you to trust me and wait out there." Dr. Jackson hoped his words burst through Baby's young mind. "And, you can leave the door open so you can see in here," he added.

Baby lowered her weapon and nodded.

"Thank you." Dr. Jackson let out a deep sigh.

Baby backpedaled out of Dr. Jackson's operating room and into the hallway. Baby stood a short distance away from the door. She had a clear view of Dr. Jackson and Treacherous. She watched as Treacherous's life lay in the hands of a total stranger.

A little over two hours had gone by, and there was still no word from the doctor. Baby's eyes grew heavy as she watched Dr. Jackson's every move. She twisted and turned in the uncomfortable plastic gray chair with cold metal hinges that held it together. Every so often, she could feel herself doze off and would jump out of her nod. The more time went by, the heavier Baby's eyes became though. She tried to shake it off a final time but sleep got the best of her. She slipped into a deep slumber.

Baby could hear Treacherous moaning in the other room from the pain. She fought with the need to leap out of the chair and run to his aid. She could hear other moans in the distance, from someone else. She turned in the direction from which the additional moans were coming. A glow from a light source produced itself from somewhere in the corner. The more intense it got, the more puzzled Baby became. She stared at it with squinted eyes. Baby could tell that something or someone was directly behind it, but she could not make the figure out. The light itself was warm and inviting. So much so that it made her uncomfortable. Baby caught a whiff of a smell, a familiar smell. She wasn't quite sure what it was but she knew she had smelled it before. The glow from the light got dimmer. She tried to walk toward it but somehow could not. She felt restrained; her whole body was attempting to move forward but something was holding it back.

"Come closer," a voice uttered.

It was a familiar voice, but she knew it couldn't be who it sounded like. Baby extended her arm in an attempt to touch the source of the voice, only to feel nothing but air. She tried again to move forward; this time she was allowed to take one step, and only one step. Suddenly, the light was gone. It was replaced by the faint sound of a rumble and rocks being thrown up against a wall or something. Just then, Baby felt liquid run down her skin. She quickly looked at it. Blood rolled down the inside of her arm. She followed its flow as it disappeared into the darkness.

Baby again attempted to take another step only to run into an object. She peered down at what seemed to be a chair. Her eyes grew wide at the sight of a pair of spread legs. Baby was baffled; she didn't know where she was and she couldn't quite figure out what was going on. Baby jumped as a hand brushed across her stomach. The touch was foreign to her. Baby tried to remove the hand but she couldn't. It was as if she was frozen still. The unfamiliar hand traveled down Baby's belly until it reached near her inner thighs. Baby's body trembled as her heart skipped every other beat. The touch of the hand had her feeling a way she had never felt before. It moved farther and farther between Baby's inner thighs until it reached its final destination. Baby's body quivered as she bit down on her bottom lip. Without thinking, she spread her legs and welcomed the unknown hand that was now massaging her clitoris. Someone was touching her where no one should have been. She thought of moving away from the hand but her body disagreed with her. She just stood there. Baby allowed the hand to make circles with her button. She began to grind her hips in a circular motion as the hand inserted two fingers inside of her. Baby threw her head back and looked up into darkness. She closed her eyes and took in the feeling of the orgasm that was building. She caressed her own neck, fiddled with her own breast, and pulled at her own nipple.

"Closer," the voice interrupted.

This time, the voice was clearer. Baby thought she may have recognized it. It belonged to a woman. Baby couldn't believe it. Guilt and shame swept through her body. Still, she could not break free of the hand. It continued to fondle Baby. You could hear the juices from her wetness coming from between her legs.

"Hi, baby girl," the voice whispered, revealing itself for the first time.

Baby cringed with fear. The voice was now unmistakably clear. Baby fought her hardest to break free of the touch. The more she struggled, the more restraint she felt. She felt a tight grip on her right shoulder. She shifted back and forth with all her might until she had finally broken free.

"Young lady. Young lady," Dr. Jackson repeated. He had been shaking Baby for the past five minutes, trying to wake her from what he believed to be a nightmare.

Baby opened her eyes to see a blurry image hovering over her. She drew her gun in record-breaking speed.

"Whoa!" Dr. Jackson threw up his hands. "You were having a nightmare of some sort," he informed her. "I was only trying to help and to see if you were okay," he added with fearful eyes.

Baby's vision had been fully restored. She cleared her throat and finally spoke. "I'm good! I'm good!" Her words came out in quick succession.

Dr. Jackson stared at her for a moment before speaking again. "Are you sure?"

"Yeah, I'm sure," Baby spat. "Now, back up! You too close." She waved the doctor off.

Dr. Jackson took a deep breath and said, "I've done all I can." He felt he had just performed the best and most memorable surgery of his life and career. He knew he would never forget that day, for many reasons.

"I hope so." She stood up. "For your sake," she added.

Dr. Jackson grimaced. "You can take him home now. I have him in a wheelchair already. You can use it to get him to the car." He didn't mind parting with the wheelchair. It was a reminder of his injury, something he felt he should have gotten rid of years ago.

"Thanks." Baby reached into her pocket and pulled out a hundred dollars.

"Keep your money." Dr. Jackson frowned. He rejected the extended hundred dollar bill. "I have a pretty strong feeling you're going to need it." He added abruptly, "Now please go." He shot Baby a look of disgust.

"Watch your fuckin' tone, muthafucka!" Baby boomed. Her gun was now pointed in Dr. Jackson's direction. Her nostrils flared.

The doctor chuckled. "I just saved your man's life and this is how you want to repay me?" he asked.

She stared at the doctor long and hard with beady eyes. She was tired of his sly remarks. She snorted and gritted her teeth. It was nothing to kill the doctor, she thought. But he was right. He had saved her man's life and didn't deserve what she may have done to him. She lowered her weapon.

"Thanks again." She shot him a smug look before she spun around and made her way into the room where Treacherous was. Minutes later, she had Treacherous secured in the car and had started putting distance between them and the veterinarian.

Now, she drove around looking for somewhere for them to lay low. The city seemed to be asleep, thought Baby as she cruised through it. It didn't look the way she had remembered it. Stores that were once thriving were now boarded up or had FOR RENT signs in the windows. This was her hometown but it didn't feel or look like it. Home was a distant memory to her. If someone were to have told her to bet money that this was how her life would turn out she would have bet every dime she owned and lost.

Her mind was racing a million miles a minute. She felt as if she were all screwed up in the head. The resentment toward her mother resurfaced at the thought. She became flustered as her thoughts traveled back to the mini episode she had back at the veterinarian's office. Her feelings were on an emotional roller coaster ride. She had never experienced anything like what she was feeling at that moment. She didn't know whether to classify what had happened as a dream or nightmare.

Her thoughts were interrupted by the neon lights that illuminated from her far left. Baby noticed the blinking sign that read CHEAP ROOMS. She hoped cheap rooms meant they'd rent to people without IDs. She knew there were places around the city that rented by the hour with no questions asked. She figured that would be perfect for them for now, just until Treacherous recuperated. She pulled the new stolen vehicle into the motel parking lot and parked a distance away from the lobby entrance. She didn't want to risk anyone seeing Treacherous laid out in the car.

As she reached the lobby door, Baby took a deep breath. She didn't want to seem suspicious or come across as overzealous. Once she felt she had it together, she entered the establishment. She was greeted with a smile.

"May I help you?" the young, freckle-faced, red-haired Caucasian male asked.

The first thing Baby noticed was the NO ID REQUIRED sign propped up on the counter. She was relieved when she saw it.

"Yes, I'd like a room."

Chapter Five

Detective Arthur Love's head rose up at the sound of rapid knocks on the other side of his office door. Although it was good to be back to work, he had given specific instructions not to be disturbed. He knew he had much to do in little time.

"Who is it?" he bellowed. The irritation was apparent in his tone.

"The police," the familiar voice replied.

Arthur Love chuckled. "Come in."

The office door swung open and in walked Andre Randle. The first thing Arthur Love noticed was the bandage he bore on the left side of his face. This was actually the first time the two of them had seen each other since the hospital.

"Good to see you, Randle," Love greeted him.

"Yeah, you too," Randle replied. The two men exchanged friendly hugs. "How are you?"

"I've seen better days, you know. Aside from being a little sore and having to use this cane from time to time, I'm good," Love concluded.

"Same here," Randle agreed. "Shoulder's a little stiff and the face is little sore. Gonna leave a nasty scar, but I'll live."

They shared agreeing smiles.

"So what's on your mind and what's the latest?" Arthur Love wasted no time asking. He was certain Andre Randle had hopped right back on the trail that landed them both in the hospital.

"This case!" Randle replied. "That's why I called," he added.

Arthur Love nodded. "Yeah, I figured. That's all I've been able to think about. Nothing else," Arthur Love confessed.

It was Andre Randle's turn to nod. "So, what you got for us?" he questioned.

"Not sure yet," Love retorted. "But the plot thickens." He shook his head.

"Talk to me." Andre Randle leaned in.

"A lot has come out while we were in the hospital." Love took a deep breath. "The old man who was killed at the pawnshop was at the top of the chain."

"I know. I saw it on the news." Randle grimaced.

"The goddamn head . . ." He paused. "Of the Irish mob," he continued with a frown plastered across his face. "Jeezus!" He shook his head. His mind was all over the place. "I mean, I knew they existed in these parts and yeah, the pawnshop had come up many times in connection to organized crime in the city." He took another deep breath. "But nobody knew that Sammy Black and the old man killed in the pawnshop were one and the same." He was now out of his chair and on his feet.

"The funny thing is I'd been hearing shit, since I was a fuckin' kid, about murders and legendary heists. There'd always been rumors and speculation about that place. A few of us never believed it was just rumors though." He placed his hands behind his back and came from behind his desk. He walked over and peered out of his office's blinds. Everything seemed to be functioning on its normal operation to him. He turned to face Randle then continued. "We had a couple of snitches here and there who claimed to know something, but before they could produce, they'd come up missing and then we'd be back to nothing." Love shook his head. "None of the locals can get any strong tips or leads to run up in there either," he added.

"That's because a place like that would have the locals paid off," Randle jumped in. "That's how that works," he stated as if he spoke the words straight out of the gospel.

"I've personally never heard of your boy Sammy Black because the mess you guys make, don't generally spill into our backyard, but we have our share of Sammy Blacks." He went on, "Any type of way somebody is getting away with committing crimes right under our nose for a lengthy period of time, some people, not only in law enforcement, are usually getting their palms greased."

"Yeah, you're right. I guess I just didn't want to believe that."

"That's because you're true blue to the shield," Andre Randle commended him.

Arthur Love nodded appreciatively. He sat back down behind his desk then drew his eyes to the paper in front of him. "Sammy Black, born Samuel Duff in Ireland, migrated to Virginia in 1962 at the young age of six. Rap sheet as a juvenile is as long as my arm, but nothing on him after that. The name, Duff, means 'black' in Irish. Ironic huh? Think that's where the name Sammy Black comes from?" He wondered.

Andre Randle was stone-faced. "Art, these fucking guys don't play," he stated.

"No shit," Love agreed. "He may not have been found guilty on anything, but this Sammy Black has been linked to some serious shit," he informed Randle. "Aside from what I've heard and already know, I've been gathering up more information about him. Been reading up on him and his family. They've been tied to everything from murder and extortion to arson and gambling. It seems like they're mostly known for gambling though," he said, drawing a conclusion. "The son, Sammy Black Jr., has been arrested, and fined on some and acquitted on other allegations of illegal gambling."

"Was anything reported stolen?"

"Of course not," Arthur Love immediately shot back. "But one of my guys was told that there was a spot set up in the back that was being used for gambling."

"So there had to be something taken." Randle grimaced. "I'll call my guys and see what I can find out."

"Yeah, because I'm sure something of value was taken. What sense would it make to hit the place and just kill this guy? Unless the kid had a vendetta against the ol' man."

"I doubt that," Randle shot down the theory. "This kid's never been outside of the seven cities prior to being admitted into the mental institution. He grew up in group homes; he didn't even know his parents until his mother kidnapped him from one of the group homes. No, that was about money and survival. I know you don't want to hear it, but your daughter could have very well heard you or somebody else talking about that spot. You said it yourself: she's a survivor and she's definitely familiar with area. Could have been her call," Randle pointed out. Any decent detective could have drawn that conclusion, so he was sure Arthur Love could see the picture. He was right.

"Yeah, that's the most logical scenario." A sharp pain jolted through Love's head. Despite all that had transpired, he did not want to believe that his daughter was the monster being hunted. "Dammit, Baby!" he yelled out. He then took a deep breath and exhaled.

Andre Randle sat and waited until Arthur Love pulled himself back together. "If what we said is the case, then not only will our guys be looking for them, Sammy Black's people will be also."

"I know, I know," Arthur Love retorted. The thought had been at the forefront of his mind all day. He'd rather his daughter spend the rest of her life in prison than be tortured, possibly raped, and killed by some cartel.

"We gotta find them before they do. Before everybody," he put emphasis on his statement to demonstrate he meant business.

"You're right," Arthur Love replied. "We may have something." Arthur Love paused. "Maybe."

"What is it?"

"White cab driver reported he was robbed by some hooker fitting the description of Baby. Said she needed a taxi and then pulled out a gun on him demanding he take her to Chamberlain and Lombardy."

"Any sign of Treacherous?"

"No, he said it was just a prostitute."

"Why would you think that was her?" Randle asked, not seeing any connection himself.

"I didn't at first. Not until the investigating officer told me how he got the taxi driver to reveal what really happened."

"I'm listening." Randle was all ears.

"Apparently, the girl was standing alongside the curb trying to flag down a taxi. He pulls up on her and rolls the window down asking does she need a taxi. She tells him yeah, but she doesn't have any money but has something else to offer. Says against his better judgment he lets her in and he makes his way to the nearest blind spot."

"So, he's confessing to solicitation?" Randle chuckled.

Love joined him in laughter. "That's the look of it. Poor guy pissed and shit himself." His laughter increased. "Admits to getting his pants open right before she popped him upside the head with a pistol, shoved him to the ground and kicked him up the ass before making him count to a thousand while she made her get-a-way."

Randle's eyes grew wide. "Are you kiddin' me?"

"Scout's honor." Love threw up the Boy Scout sign with his two fingers.

Randle shook his head in disbelief. He still had the grin on his face from laughing. "You think that was her scoring another car." It was more of a statement than question.

"Possible." Love nodded. "We're waiting on a call now as to the whereabouts of the taxi. It has a tracking device on it. We should be—" Before he could finish his sentence, a second knock on his office door interrupted him. "Yes!"

The door opened and young white male officer appeared. "Sir, they've located the taxi."

Arthur Love and Andre Randle looked at each other.

"Where?" He directed his attention back to the officer.

"Parked in the parking lot of a convenience store off of Chamberlain and Lombardy."

"What's the status?"

"Forensics is headed over now for prints and DNA."

"Thank you, Officer."

The officer backpedaled out of the office and closed the door behind him.

"Time to go to work," Arthur Love announced.

"You took the words right out of my mouth," Andre Randle agreed.

Chapter Six

Swimming in the two-hundred-foot-long indoor pool always relaxed Sammy Black Jr. He gently backstroked the length of the pool, as he calmly breathed in and out of his nostrils. His Irish homeland anthem filled the air. It added to his relaxation. He enjoyed everything about his swim sessions. Lately he had been swimming more often than usual. It was the only thing that kept him from going out and taking his anger and rage for the loss of his father out on somebody else until he tracked down those responsible. It was all surreal for him. He knew that day would come when he would be afforded the opportunity to become his father's successor. The other families' primary concern was retrieving the duffle bags but that was secondary to Sammy Jr. His primary mission was to avenge his father's death. The thought caused him to swim even faster and more aggressively. He swam until he exhausted himself. Fortunately, this was right before he reached the end of the pool. As he floated to the edge of the pool, he was met with a towel. He climbed out of the water and began to dry off.

"It's not much, but we got something," Big Lou greeted his boss.

"What is it?" Sammy Jr. dropped the towel from his face and cut his eyes over at Big Lou.

"A friend of ours at the station said they tracked down a second getaway car in Richmond, possibly to the robbers. Said he'd let us know for sure after forensics confirms."

"So, the idiots are still local." He gritted his teeth.

"It seems so." Big Lou shook his head.

"That's good. Really good," he repeated.

"Yeah, we need to catch these niggers," Big Lou chimed. "The sooner the better," he added.

Don't worry, we will. "Did my cousin get here yet?" he abruptly asked.

"They have him en route now. And all of our guys are on point. Everybody knows what time to be here. We're good, buddy," Lou assured his boss and childhood friend.

"Thanks, Lou." He nodded.

Big Lou had been his only friend and had his back ever since they were kids. On many occasions, Big Lou had put his life and reputation on the line to protect and defend him. He had taken a knife to the gut in a pub brawl after a guy made the mistake of calling Sammy Jr. a yellow coward when they were teenagers, right before he had snapped the guy's neck and had caught a bullet to the chest during a hijacking gone wrong because Sammy Jr. forgot to pat the driver down. It was Sammy Jr. who had actually planted the bullet in the driver's head after he'd shot Big Lou. The two had each other's back from day one.

"Don't mention it, boss; he was like a father to me too," Big Lou retorted.

Sammy Jr. continued to nod. He knew the effect and influence his father had on the men around him and in their organization. It was the same memory Sammy Jr. intended to leave with the family as well. Starting with the way he handled this matter.

"Let me know when everybody gets here," Sammy Jr. said then made his way over to the minibar.

Chapter Seven

Treacherous's eyelids flickered. He tried to open them but was unsuccessful. The cold in them made it feel as if they were glued together. His mouth was dry and his throat felt like sandpaper. He felt weak and heavy as if something had him restrained or tied down. Something had him feeling sluggish and lightheaded. The smell of stale cigarettes tickled his nostrils. He knew he didn't know anybody who smoked. *Have I been caught?* he wondered. He was determined to find out where he was. *Where's Baby?* was his next thought.

He fought to pry his eyelids open from the cold that had formed around them. When he finally got them open the first thing he noticed was the familiar once white but now beige ceiling. He hoped he wasn't dead. For a split second the thought frightened him. He shook it off though. The only other explanation he could come up with was that he was dreaming. He immediately x-ed out that idea when he shifted his body weight. A sharp pain shot through his chest when he attempted to rise up. He knew there was no way he was dreaming with the kind of pain he had just felt. It felt as if someone had hit him in the chest with a sledgehammer and kicked him in the lower back at the same time. He nearly lost his breath when a spasm jolted through his body. He immediately lay back. He opened and closed his eyes repeatedly until they were completely free from what held them captive. The first thing he saw was the image standing in front of his view. He couldn't make out the figure and still was no closer to finding out where he was or how he had gotten there. But a familiar voice immediately put him at ease.

"How you feelin'?" a relieved Baby asked. She had been watching over him for nearly seventy-two hours.

A smile slowly appeared on Treacherous's face. "Sore." His voice was groggy from the dryness of his throat. A sharp pain shot through his forehead causing a throbbing headache that had Excedrin written all over it. He attempted to raise himself up for a second time. Only this time he used his arms for assistance. He balled his fists and pressed them down into the queen-sized bed. Baby pressed her hand up against his chest.

"You should be sore. You've been out of commission for a couple of days now. Save your strength. We're safe for now. We're just outside of Richmond," Baby answered.

"Where are we?" Treacherous looked around. He scanned the room. Something caught his eye. He noticed the cockroach scurrying up the wall past a smoke detector that was missing from the space on the wall where it should have been. He watched as the cockroach disappeared into a hole in the wall that appeared more like someone's fist print than just a regular hole. Baby glanced over and saw what Treacherous had zeroed in on. She just shook her head. She had been stepping on and crushing the bugs with her shoe for the past few days since they had been holed up in the dingy room. Treacherous drew his attention back to Baby, who stood next to an old prehistoric box television and small, round table propped up next to the room's window. If nothing else, those were was a dead giveaway for Treacherous that they were in a motel.

"It was the best I could do, under the circumstances." Baby could practically read his mind. Treacherous had no recollection as to how they had gotten to the motel or how long they had even been there. He actually couldn't remember much of anything. The next thing he noticed was the bandage on the left side of his chest and dressing wrapped around his right arm.

"What happened?"

"You were shot, remember?" Baby offered.

A flashback instantly appeared in Treacherous's head. His jaws clenched at the thought.

An image of the detective invaded his young mind. The incident and all that had taken place back at Baby's house was still a little foggy but there was no mistaking who the shooter was.

"Muthafucka, agh!" Treacherous chimed. His sudden reaction caused a sharp pain to jolt across his chest.

"I know, baby, but you gotta relax. The doctor, rather the vet, said you needed to rest and that you'd be fine. He removed the bullets and gave you something to help with the pain." Baby let out a light chuckle as she spoke. Her words broke Treacherous's train of thought. The look on Treacherous's face was priceless. His expression went from anger to confusion. She knew he didn't understand.

"Boo, I had no choice," she started out. "I couldn't risk taking you to a regular hospital, so I did the next best thing. It was either let the veterinarian work on you, take you to Richmond General and let them lock you up afterward, or watch you die, and that was not an option."

Treacherous bore a blank stare. He was still processing Baby's words. "You took me to an animal doctor?" Treacherous shook his head.

"Bae—"

"It's okay," Treacherous interjected. "I probably would have done the same thing." A half grin appeared across Treacherous's face. He found Baby's hand and took hold of it. "I love you." He raised Baby's hand to his mouth and kissed the back of it.

"I love you too." Baby returned his words. She leaned in, planted a kiss on Treacherous's forehead, and then made her way to his lips. The kiss was quick but the energy was electrifying. A tear managed to escape from the crease of Baby's right eye. She couldn't imagine what life would have been like had she lost the one person she truly loved.

She curled up under Treacherous and rested her head on his chest.

"So how bad was it?" Treacherous asked.

"The bullet was close to your heart." She told Treacherous what was told to her by the vet. "Between how long it took me to find a secure place and the vet going in to get the bullet, you lost a lot of blood. I thought I was going to lose you," she admitted through sniffles.

"I'm not going anywhere anytime soon," Treacherous replied. He caressed her hair and kissed her on top of her head.

Baby smiled.

"At least, not until we finish what we started!" Treacherous recanted.

Baby peered up at him. "I'm with you!" She stared into Treacherous's eyes. At that moment, there were no words that needed to be spoken. Ride or die were their only options. The look in their eyes and the dead silence in the room spoke volumes.

"I'm starving," Treacherous chimed out of nowhere.

"Yeah, you need to eat," Baby agreed. "I have some lunch meat and stuff in an ice bucket. You want me to make you a sandwich?"

"Anything, I don't care." Treacherous attempted to rise up for a second time.

Baby could hear his stomach growling through the motel blanket. She climbed off the bed and made her way over to the sink area where the ice bucket was located.

Treacherous watched as she sashayed over to the area. Something on the table caught his eye. It was one thing to see it bundled up in the bags, but to see the stack of bills piled up was a very different ball game. Treacherous knew they had scored a nice amount of money back at the pawnshop that they had robbed. But at the time, it hadn't appeared to be as much as it did now that he saw it like this. Just then, Treacherous noticed that the larger of the two bags they had taken had not been opened.

"Did you count it?" he asked.

Baby turned around, nodded, and smiled. "Yes, I did." She beamed. Her reaction told Treacherous she was pleased with the amount.

"How much?" he wanted to know.

"$258,000. Well . . ." She paused. "Fifty-four, because I took out some and bought us a car from a private owner, a little ol' black lady who lives on a farm way out in the sticks, for $2,500 no questions asked. She told me that her husband died a few years back and the car had been sitting. She said it brought back too many memories and she just wanted to get rid of it. She even trusted me to turn in the plates on the car once I got it transferred over. So, that should buy us some time. She was a very nice lady," Baby accounted. "And, I got us some clothes, food, and other miscellaneous things we needed, but the last time I counted it, that was the count," she said. "I've been counting it for the past three days." She paused. "Both bags," she added.

You could see the excitement in Treacherous's eyes. This reminded him of a scene he had read in his mother's journals about her and his father. That was more than enough to put some distance between them and Virginia, he thought.

"What's in the other bag?" Treacherous asked.

"That's what I've been waiting to show you." Baby came walking over with two turkey and cheese sandwiches wrapped in a napkin along with a room-temperature bottled water. She handed Treacherous the food and drink then scurried over to retrieve the bag.

She plopped herself and the bag onto the bed as Treacherous smacked away. He devoured the first sandwich and bottled water in less than a minute. He had just bitten into the second sandwich when Baby unzipped the bag.

"What's that?" he asked, peering into the bag.

"Chips," Baby enlightened him.

"Chips?" Treacherous was not following.

"Casino chips," Baby continued.

"What do you mean?" Treacherous was still clueless.

"What I mean is that the rumors about that pawnshop were true," Baby retorted. "These casino chips are worth a lot of money." She pulled out a handful as she spoke. "I mean a lot of money!" she repeated.

Treacherous could see the number amounts on the few chips in Baby's hand. $100 and $500 was mostly what he saw. He believed there was one that had $1,000 on it.

"How much? Treacherous wanted to know.

"Casino value, I counted $2.5 million."

He nearly spit the chewed-up sandwich out of his mouth. "Two point—"

"Yes." Baby smiled and nodded. She cut him off before he could repeat what she had told him. "And in the streets they're probably worth half, if we knew somebody who knew anything about these."

"That's a lot of money," Treacherous announced.

"I was thinking the same thing." Baby joined him. "Which means we really have another problem on our hands," Baby pointed out.

"I didn't think it could get any worse than it already is." Treacherous grimaced.

"Well, it can," Baby corrected him. "These casino chips prove the stories about the store being a front. But I never told you who I heard it was a front for." Baby frowned. Her facial expression concerned Treacherous. She took a deep breath. "The Irish mob." She stared Treacherous in the eyes. She waited for his reaction. He had none. He was still processing what Baby had said.

"We need to get out of this motel and find a better place to lay our heads," Treacherous stated.

Baby nodded in agreement. "I've already been checking out some places on the outskirts."

"That's cool, but eventually we need to get the hell out of VA," Treacherous chimed. "If what you're saying is true, then somebody's gonna come looking for this money and these chips," Treacherous made Baby aware. By the grace of God, they had escaped some serious gun battles and managed to evade the law by the skin of their teeth, but Treacherous didn't think he and Baby were built for or equipped to go up against the mob.

Baby let Treacherous's words marinate. She hadn't really given the thought any mind. Now that he had made her aware, the reality of what they had in their possession dawned on her.

"I agree," Baby concurred. "We have to get out of Virginia until we can figure out our next move," she added.

"Yeah, but where?" Treacherous shot back.

"Don't worry, I got us," Baby assured him. In her mind, she was already thinking of possible places to consider laying low. Once she secured that she intended to make a to-do list while Treacherous was recuperating.

"Yeah, I got us," Baby repeated with a smile...

Chapter Eight

Detective Love and Randle pulled into the minimart and parked. "So, this is how Richmond's finest does it, huh?" Randle joked. The area in which the taxi was discovered was blocked off with crime scene tape. Uniformed and plainclothes officers flooded the area. One would have thought it was the scene of a homicide.

Arthur Love chuckled. "Just doing their job, Chief," Love retorted. "We know we don't got nothing on you big city folk," he shot back.

"Touché." Randle chuckled at Love's snappy comeback. The two men exited the vehicle.

"What's up, Mike?" Detective Love greeted his colleague, who was standing by an unmarked car.

"Hey, Art." Senior Detective Mike Johnson turned around. The two men shook hands. They had known each other for over ten years. Mike Johnson had graduated the academy two classes ahead of Arthur Love and outranked him.

"This is Chief Andre Randle from the Norfolk PD," Love introduced. Whenever he gave Randle's title, he felt awkward saying it to his peers, knowing that he was not on active duty anymore, but was actually retired. Love shook the feeling off. There were more important things to be concerned about, he concluded. He watched as both men nodded and shook hands.

"You in charge?"

"Yup," Detective Mike Johnson confirmed.

"What you got?" Detective Love wanted to know.

There was a dead silence for a moment. "Art, I can get my ass chewed for this." Detective Johnson paused. "You know, with it being a personal matter for you and all."

"Listen, Mike. I'm shield first, above all," Detective Love announced boldly. "I'm not asking you to hand the case over to me," he added.

Detective Johnson scratched the top of his head. "Hasn't been confirmed yet, but if I had to say, it was definitely them," he offered.

"Appreciate that," Detective Love retorted. "But, why do you think it's them?"

"We found traces of blood in the back seat. Could be one of theirs. It says one if not both of them may be wounded in the case file. Just waiting on ballistics."

"Good job, Mike, and thanks ag—" Before he could finish his sentence another officer joined them.

"Hello, sir." He directed his words to Love. Detective Love nodded.

"What is it?" Detective Johnson asked.

"We just got word from the station that a call came in from a veterinarian."

Puzzled looks appeared on the faces of the three men as the officer spoke. "He reported that he removed a bullet from a man's chest a few days ago. Just now deciding to call in about it, said he was afraid for his life."

Both Love and Randle looked at each other.

"So, he has a dead man in his office now?" Detective Johnson asked in an irritated tone.

Both Arthur Love and Randle knew Senior Detective Johnson didn't make the connection they had.

"No, the man lived, sir. A woman took him out of there after he finished operating on the man. He said the woman held him at gunpoint."

It wasn't until the officer ended that Mike Johnson put the pieces of the puzzle together. "Got you."

"They wanted you to send someone over to investigate it." The officer handed Detective Mike Johnson a piece of paper. "That's the address," the officer announced.

Detective Arthur Love moved in closer. He didn't utter a word. Instead he just stood there and stared at Mike Johnson. Senior Detective Mike Johnson shook his head in defeat. "Here, take it!"

"I owe you one." Love beamed. "No, I owe you two," he corrected himself.

Chapter Nine

Treacherous struggled to make his way to the bathroom. With each step, he let out a light grunt. The pain in his chest brought him discomfort, but the spasms in his lower back had him hunched over like the hunchback of Notre Dame. Baby had offered her help but he declined. He knew if he wanted to recover quickly he had to push himself.

He eased the shower curtain back and reached over to turn the shower on. When he pulled it back he saw a spider resting on the shower's handle. He flicked the spider off the handle then turned the water on and adjusted its temperature. Once satisfied, he slowly climbed in and positioned himself underneath the showerhead in a way in which the water would not hit him directly on the chest.

The hot water beating up against his flesh was just what Treacherous needed. He turned around and let it serve as a back massager. It felt as if he were being massaged by thousands of little warm hands. After about five minutes, he turned back around. He lathered his body with soap, careful not to get any on his bandages. He then repositioned his body, slid his head under the stream of water, and closed his eyes. He then stretched his arm until his shoulders were directly under the shower-head, and he placed his hand on the wall for support. The little motel shower made it difficult for his wide frame.

A funny feeling on his fingers caused his eyes to shoot open. When he looked up he noticed he had placed his hand in the spider's web up in the far right corner of the shower. It sat right below some built-up mildew. He shook his head at the conditions he and Baby had to deal with. He peered down at the wound. The veterinarian had left an L-shaped incision just off to the right of his left pectoral. Treacherous ran his hand across the stitches protruding from his chest. He realized how blessed he was to be alive. He also thought about how blessed he was to have someone like Baby in his life and corner. In a short period of time, she had proven she was the type of woman he had read about his mother being. Treacherous truly believed he had found his ride or die chick. The love he felt for Baby was indescribable to him.

I love this girl to death. She's the one.

His mind was abruptly interrupted by the touch of a hand around his semi-erect dick. Treacherous opened his eyes. He was in such deep thought that he never heard her enter the bathroom.

When Baby slid the curtain back she couldn't help but admire the sculpture of his body. For a moment she just stood there staring, watching him with his eyes closed and his head under the water. She began to feel tingly inside. She could feel her now moist cat throbbing as she gazed at his dick. Without warning, she leaned in and gently grabbed hold of it. She smiled when his eyes shot open as she stroked his manhood. It grew rock hard in her hand. She could feel it pulsating.

She stepped into the shower, moved in closer toward him, and raised up on her tippy toes until she was staring into his eyes. The average person would have only seen his mesmerizing brown eyes, but Baby saw more than that. She saw love in them. A love she believed he only had for her. She pressed her lips up against his. Treacherous embraced the kiss by parting her lips with his tongue. They became one as the two passionately battled in a lip lock. They exchanged breaths as their heartbeats danced to the same rhythmic beat.

The kiss seemed to last forever. It wasn't until Treacherous felt water cascading down his shoulder and onto his chest that he freed himself of their lip lock His bandages were getting wet. "Let's get out," he suggested. He took hold of Baby's hand and guided her out of the shower. They dripped their way out of the bathroom until they were faced with the motel bed. Baby gazed into Treacherous's eyes. She lightly shoved him onto the bed and slithered her way between his legs. She never broke her stare. She took Treacherous into her mouth. She tightened her lips around the helmet of his dick then slid them lower and lower. He arched his back and braced himself on the bed as she swallowed him whole. Baby's lips, tongue, and tonsils pulsated around his length. It was driving him crazy. Treacherous restrained as long as he could but couldn't take it any longer. The tingling sensation came without warning.

"Agh," he let out, as he exploded like TNT.

Baby continued sucking on him. She took every bit of his juices until there were none left. Treacherous looked down at her. Baby had a devilish grin plastered across her beautiful face.

"I love you," she cooed.

"I love you too," Treacherous replied. He rose up and lifted Baby off the floor. He positioned her onto the bed and grabbed hold of her right leg. He kissed the toes of her size seven, and then did the same with the left. He then grabbed Baby by the waist and pulled her to the edge of the bed. He parted her legs to fit his frame then buried his face between them. His tongue took a tour into Baby's sex tunnel. He lifted her clitoral hood with his tongue then sucked on it like it was an oyster. Baby's toes curled as the electrifying sensation traveled throughout her body. His tongue probed Baby. She grabbed hold of his head and clamped down. Treacherous slid his tongue upward until it reached Baby's clit again. He wrapped his lips around it and began to gently suck and kiss on it.

Baby's body began to quiver. She felt like her insides were about to explode. The fire she felt building up in her stomach had her going crazy. She was in heaven. Sweat trickled down her brow and the veins in her neck protruded as she arched her back in ecstasy. She bit down on her bottom lip. It seemed like with every second the fire inside her kept building. She raised her legs and wrapped them around Treacherous's neck. She began grinding her hips counterclockwise. Treacherous continued to tongue sex her as Baby rode his face. He took the pain that he was feeling from all of Baby's movements like a champ. It was worth it, he thought. It was his every intent to please Baby in all ways possible. He knew he was doing that now.

Baby's love box was so wet her juices ran down her glistening thighs and soaked into the mattress. Baby was panting and moaning softly. Her body was in shock. "Yes," Baby cried out. Treacherous put his palms underneath Baby's voluptuous ass and pulled her body closer to him. He continued flicking his tongue up and down her clitoris at a feverish pace.

"Ohh, I'm about to cum again!" Baby bellowed.

Hearing that, Treacherous slowed his pace. Baby released her death lock from around Treacherous's neck. He tasted her juices then began planting light kisses between her inner thighs.

He was now ready to feel himself inside of Baby. Treacherous rose up. He took his middle finger and began massaging Baby's outer walls then slipped it inside of her. Baby tensed up. Out of nowhere, her mood changed.

Treacherous grabbed hold of his length. He guided himself between Baby's legs. Baby stopped him in mid-motion. Her inner thighs locked up on his outer thighs.

"What's wrong?" Treacherous looked up at her. He noticed she was crying.

"Baby, what's wrong?" he asked again seeing her tears. A concerned look appeared across his face.

"Nothing," she replied through sniffles.

"What do you mean, nothing!" Treacherous threw back at her. "You lying here crying and you expect me to believe that, huh? Now tell me what's wrong." Treacherous's words came out in a barrage. He knew Baby was lying to him and he wanted to know why.

"I don't know!" Baby cried. "I don't know! I don't fucking know!" she repeated. "I don't know what the fuck is wrong with me!" Baby became hysterical. Treacherous hadn't seen her act like that since they were at the mental institution.

He didn't know what to do. He went with his instincts and did what he felt was the best thing to do. Treacherous grabbed hold of Baby and blanketed her in his arms.

By now Baby's cries had grown. But the warmth of Treacherous's body soothed her and made her feel safe. It reminded her of why she loved him so much in the first place. Baby buried her face in Treacherous's chest. She knew what was wrong with her. She was just embarrassed to say. But she trusted Treacherous. She trusted him with her life. *He deserves to know,* she reasoned with herself. *Fuck it, I'ma just tell him,* she decided.

Baby rose up. Treacherous massaged his chest in a circular motion after releasing her.

"Did I hurt you?" she asked with concern in her tone.

"Nah, I'm straight," he assured her. "You good?" he asked.

A nervous look appeared on Baby's face. She closed her eyes and opened them back up quickly to evade the image that haunted her thoughts. She took a deep breath. She didn't know where to begin, so she just blurted out the first thing that came to mind.

"That shit with my mother got me fucked up in the head."

"I know but—"

"No, let me finish," Baby interrupted him. "You don't know, because I don't even fuckin' know," she continued. "But when you put your finger in me it did something to me," Baby confessed. She didn't know how to tell him what thoughts had been triggered. "I don't know why I'm having these fuckin' feelings." Baby wiped the tears that spilled out of her eyes.

A puzzled look appeared across Treacherous's face. "What feelings?" he wanted to know.

Baby took another deep breath. "Feelings about . . ." She paused. "Being with another woman!"

The words spat out of her mouth like venom. Treacherous didn't know what to say. That was not something he was expecting to hear, or even thought to be what was wrong with Baby. He just stared at Baby in silence.

"Aren't you going to say something?" Baby asked him.

"So, what do you want to do?" Treacherous replied.

That made Baby laugh. "What the fuck you mean, what do I want to do?" she repeated his question.

"Just what I said: what do you want to do about how you're feeling?" Treacherous stood his ground. "Because whatever you want to do, I'm with you." He ended.

Baby stared at him long and hard. *This nigga is ahead of his time.* Baby smiled on the inside. She had never heard anything more real than the words Treacherous had spoken to her. Here it was: he was willing to stand by her side and hold her hand while she figured out her sexual preference. The thought of it filled Baby's stomach with butterflies. *I would ride with him to the end of the earth,* she told herself.

"Thank you." Baby smiled. "I'll work it out."

"Don't thank me. And nah, we'll work it out. Together," Treacherous corrected her.

Baby felt like a schoolgirl. For the first time in a long time she blushed.

"You're right. We will. Together," she repeated.

Chapter Ten

Sammy Black Jr. entered the chatter-filled room. He did a survey of the faces in attendance. Pretty much everyone he expected to be there was, in fact, in the room sitting at the table. Cuban cigar smoke filled the air. The smell of Scotch tickled his nose. He was in need of another drink and a Cuban himself. Once his crew realized he was in the room, the chatter began to die down. He had called an emergency meeting and all of the members were all too curious to know the nature of the unexpected gathering.

He made his way over to the bar. He dropped two ice cubes in a glass and filled it halfway with Scotch. He then clipped the end of a Cuban and lit it. He took a swig of the liquor on the rocks as he walked over and positioned himself at the head of the table. He couldn't help but watch the people he considered family in the room. The room was filled with men who had laid their lives on the line and would do it again and again in the blink of an eye for him and his family.

He knew calling the emergency meeting would have all of them on high alert and that's exactly what he wanted. He knew how much they all loved and respected his father. He wanted them all to be motivated and charged up about finding the couple responsible for the loss of their deceased boss, and bring them to him. He wanted his men to put the full-court press on the streets until they brought the killers out of hiding or until they slipped up. Most importantly, he wanted them all to know he would be running the organization with the same iron fist as his father.

He put his thoughts on hold when he saw who he had been expecting. Everybody's attention was drawn to the new arrival who had just entered the room. Sammy Black Jr. just smiled.

"Sorry I'm late," Joshua Black announced. He peered over at his cousin. He returned Sammy Jr.'s smile. He then replaced it with a more solemn, apologetic one for being tardy. Sammy Jr. acknowledged him with a nod. Aside from him being his boss, he was his favorite cousin. Although the two were first cousins, they were more like brothers. Sammy Jr.'s father was also Joshua's favorite uncle and like a father to him as well. Which was why when he got the call from Sammy Black Jr. about the death of his father and requested that he come back to the East Coast, Joshua Black dropped everything and headed to LAX Airport.

Joshua found a corner and wasted no time posting up in it. He nodded in Big Lou's direction. Everybody made it their business to show Joshua Black some form of respect. His name rang bells from Ireland to America in their world. He may have been only five foot one, 143 pounds, but his reputation was that of a colossus. Every man in the room knew at least one legendary tale about Joshua Black. The one known to all was how he single-handedly wiped out an entire crew who had been trying to muscle their way in on their family's business when Sammy Black Sr. was still alive. It was reported that over a dozen dead bodies were discovered in the Richmond mansion. The allegation was the reason why Joshua Black was sent to California, until the heat died down. That was nearly ten years ago.

"Glad everybody could make it," Sammy Jr. announced. He threw the remainder of his drink back then made himself another. That instantly drew the attention of his crew. It wasn't too often that they saw their leader toss drinks back like that. They all knew the only time he actually drank excessively was when they were either celebrating or he was about to put some work in. Everybody sat attentively waiting for Sammy Jr. to fill them in on why they were all there.

He chose his words wisely before he spoke. "We have a serious situation," he informed the room. Everybody in the room began to nod. They were well aware of the situation. They all waited, eager to know what their new leader would say next.

"We need to nip this in the bud immediately!" Sammy Jr. boomed. Judging by the looks on their faces, he knew what was going on in everybody's mind. "These pieces of shit didn't just take one of our own; they took a piece of our heart!" Sammy Jr. continued. "And there's no getting it back!" He let his words linger for a moment.

By now, he had his crew on edge and charged up. "Aside from the life of my father, they also took something else very valuable from us," Sammy Jr. added.

There had been a lot of rumors floating among the other families as to what was really taken, but no one knew for sure. Everybody in the room listened attentively. They all wanted to know.

"Over $3 million has been stolen." Sammy shook his head in disgust. His words caused murmurs and chatter among the other families. He noticed everybody in the room shaking their heads, as well. The room was now in an uproar. Surprised expressions were plastered across everyone's faces. Sammy Jr. knew he had to say something to gain order within the room.

"A hundred grand goes to the one who tracks them down first." His words raised eyebrows and eased the room a bit. "Now, this shit can't be taken lightly. I'm sure you can understand my concern and anger." He let his words linger and marinate. "It's not just about me; it's about us. Our family reputation is on the line. For decades this family has been handling anything that comes our way and if somebody jeopardizes what we stand for, examples are made." Sammy Jr.'s words triggered an uproar of agreement. He watched the reaction of every member. This was the state of mind he wanted them all to be in. "I want them alive," he added with emphasis. His statement brought silence into the room. No one dared to say a word.

"Do what you have to do to track them down, but no one is to take matters into their own hands." Sammy Jr. wanted to be sure he was clear on his instructions.

One by one, his crew gave agreeing nods.

"Good." *First mission accomplished.* "I know it's late, so I'm not gonna prolong this meeting any further," he concluded. "Now, let's make my dad proud and find these sons of bitches!" he ended abruptly.

No one uttered a word. Instead they all rose up out of their seats. One by one they gave Sammy Jr. hugs as they began to exit the room. Moments later, the room was nearly empty. The ones remaining in the room were Sammy Black Jr. and Joshua Black. The words Sammy Black Jr. intended to say were for his cousin's ears only.

Chapter Eleven

The sound of an array of dogs barking filled the air as Love and Randle stepped foot on the porch of the veterinarian hospital.

"May I help you?"

"Dr. Peter Jackson?" Love asked.

"Yes."

"I'm Detective Love and this is Detective Randle. We're from the Richmond PD," Arthur Love partially lied. He thought it was best that he say Andre Randle was a Richmond police officer rather than Norfolk PD. He retrieved his wallet and flashed his badge at who he believed to be the doctor.

"Oh yes, I'm sorry, please excuse me," Dr. Jackson apologized. The truth was ever since the incident with Baby and Treacherous he was leery of all new faces. The fact that they were black and in plain clothes didn't help the matter either. He was still bothered by the fact that he had escaped becoming a statistic and made it out of the ghetto through education and serving his country, only to have what he came from come to his front door. He took a more thorough look at Randle and Love. "Either of you serve?" he asked.

"Only law enforcement," Love answered. Randle followed up with a head nod.

Dr. Jackson believed the two men were actual police officers. "You're still protecting our country." He opened the door and invited the detectives in. "Excuse the noise," Dr. Jackson said in reference to the barking.

"No problem," both men sang in unison.

Once sitting in his office, Dr. Jackson rewound his mental tapes and played them back to the detectives of his run-in with who they believed to be Treacherous and Baby.

"So, what about the girl?" Love asked. "She didn't need any medical attention?"

"If she did, I didn't treat her," Dr. Jackson replied.

Love was hopeful after hearing the doctor's response to his question. "Thank you for your time. If we come across anything we'll let you know. Sorry for your inconvenience." The two detectives stood up.

"Thank you, guys, for stopping by." Dr. Jackson flashed a friendly smile. He saw the detectives to the door.

"It's definitely them," Arthur Love was the first to say once outside and out of earshot of the doctor.

"No doubt about it," Randle agreed. "And he's badly hurt, so that confirms the blood in the taxi," he added.

"Yeah," was all Arthur Love said. His mind was elsewhere. Despite all that had happened it was still difficult for him not to be a concerned parent. All he could think about was how relieved he was to hear that his daughter was not hurt, when he knew he should have been focusing on gathering information so that she and her boyfriend could be brought to justice.

Chapter Twelve

"You sure this is the right room?" Joshua Black asked Frank McNitty, looking at the motel room key he had just been handed.

"I'm positive, 148, 'round back." The young swimmer-built Irish kid by the name of Frank McNitty nodded. His deep green eyes shifted toward the right of him as he pointed. "I'm not sure if they're who you're looking for, but according to the description given to me by Rudy at my school, I'm almost for sure it's them," he added.

He felt flustered and his words came out a little nervously. His freckled face nearly matched his bushy red hair now. Looking at Joshua Black confirmed his opinion about the person who told him how he could earn some cash. When he'd first heard from Rudy, an Irish kid he always thought to be bad news, about a reward for information on a couple fitting the description of the suspicious black couple staying at the motel he worked at, he was reluctant to entertain it. Had it not been for his financial struggles he wouldn't have even considered inquiring more. But between trying to pay for his student loans and take care of his mother and little sister, he was desperate. When he found out the reward would be $25,000 dollars, it was a no-brainer for him. Now he was that much closer to the money he so needed. In his mind he had already spent the money. He had reasoned with himself that if someone was willing to pay that type of money for the whereabouts of the black couple then they must have done something really bad. That was his way of having no remorse, and his excuse not to have a guilty conscience.

Joshua Black studied Frank McNitty. "I'll be right back." He then announced, "If everything pans out, you'll get what's owed to you." He relayed to the young Irish kid what was relayed to him when he'd first received instructions to check out the lead given to them by Rudy, one of Sammy's young street thugs.

Frank McNitty nodded in rapid succession. Joshua Black turned and exited the motel lobby. He hopped in his sedan and drove around to the back of the motel. The room numbers started in the 160s, counting down. Joshua Black pulled over and parked.

His eyes shifted from his side-view to rearview mirrors. He checked his surroundings before exiting the car. The coast seemed clear. Just as he was about to open his door, a couple came staggering out of one of the rooms a few doors down. Luckily for him, they were too busy groping and kissing one another to notice him sitting in his car. He waited as the two lovebirds bent the corner and vanished. He was met with a foul stench when he climbed out of his vehicle. The smell was a mixture of second-hand smoke, urine, and old leftovers. He withdrew his handkerchief and held it up to his face. Moments later, he stood in front of room 148. He drew his silencer-equipped 9 mm and placed his ear up against the door.

The muffled sound of the news on television could be heard playing on the other side of the motel room door. He listened a few seconds more before pulling out the electronic room key and inserting it. The light turned green. Joshua Black pushed down lightly on the door handle and gently opened the motel room door. He wasted no time waving his gun around the room. It only took a couple of seconds to realize he had nearly shot up an empty room. He entered the room and let the door close behind him.

The first thing he noticed was how spotless the room appeared. There was nothing in the room that indicated anybody had been in it. There was no trash, used towels or washcloths, or personal items anywhere in sight. It was easy for him to draw the conclusion that whoever occupied the room did not any longer. He walked over toward the bed, snatched the linen off, and flipped up the mattress, hoping for a clue or something to go off of. He came up empty. He released the mattress and let it fall back onto its box spring. Something appeared from under the bed as the mattress landed, causing him to look down. A sinister grin appeared across his face as he kneeled.

He rose up and made his way to the motel room door. His work was done there. The casino chip belonging to the families was all he needed to confirm that who he was looking for had in fact been there. He let himself out the way he had come in and made his way back to the front desk.

Frank McNitty's eyes grew with excitement when he saw Joshua Black returning. "So, is it them?" he asked.

"Yes," Joshua Black replied.

Frank McNitty couldn't hold back his smile.

"But they're gone," Joshua Black added.

Frank McNitty's smile instantly turned into a frown. The familiar beet-red look returned from earlier. "Aww fuck!" he cursed. "So, what does that mean? I don't get the reward?" The disappointment could be heard in his tone.

"I'm afraid it means your services are no longer need-ed," Joshua Black clarified.

Frank McNitty never saw him draw his weapon from behind his back. By the time he saw the small hole of the silencer pointing in his direction, it was too late. The bullet penetrated his skull, sending him tumbling back. Joshua Black came around the corner and put one more shot in his head. He looked around until he located what he was looking for. Once he spotted the recorders, he wasted no time retrieving the video surveillance tapes. He then stuffed the four discs in his jacket pocket then calmly exited the motel lobby for a second time and pulled onto the main road.

Chapter Thirteen

Meanwhile, thirty-five minutes away from Richmond . . .

Butterflies danced in Baby's stomach as she pulled onto the stone-filled driveway. She had no way of knowing what she had just evaded back at the motel.

"We're here." She turned and looked at Treacherous. She nervously watched as Treacherous took in the scenery. She took a deep breath then exited the driver's side of the vehicle. She made her way over to the passenger's side. She made an attempt to help Treacherous out of the car. He waved her off.

"I got it," Treacherous announced.

"Okay." She smiled proudly. She let him be and walked toward the door of where she had just pulled up to. "So, this is it." She introduced their new place.

Baby had been running around for the past few days getting everything situated for the two of them. She wanted everything to be perfect. It meant everything to her that her lover approved of every move she made on behalf of them. Baby's anxiety grew for the big reveal as Treacherous exited the car. It wasn't that she thought he'd be disappointed at her choice, she just wanted to show him that she would always have his back and that he could trust her judgment if they were ever apart. It was important to Baby that he knew that. He had proven his loyalty to her time and time again without even trying and she wanted to reciprocate. Although they weren't bound by marriage, Baby had vowed to ride through sickness and health and for better or worse. Now, here it was: they officially stood outside of what would be their first official place to call home.

The first thing Treacherous noticed when he climbed out of the car was how quiet the neighborhood was. It was so quiet you could hear a needle drop in a haystack. All that could be heard were crickets chirping and a variety of hissing noises made by whatever lurked in the grass and trees. A sense of peace swept through Treacherous's body. In the midst of all that they were dealing with, the area made him feel safe. The neighborhood sort of reminded him of the area Baby had grown up in. He could see why she had picked the one-family house she'd rented for them.

The neighborhood was the perfect place to hide out, thought Baby. She was surprised to have found the vacancy in the want ads section of the newspaper. After viewing three other properties, Baby knew the crib thirty-five minutes on the outskirts of Richmond was the right choice. Houses were spaced out miles apart, and there was no heavy foot or flow of traffic, so they didn't have to worry about nosey neighbors or good Samaritans passing by. It was the type of area where the only people you'd see around were the people who lived there.

Treacherous made his way to the front door of the house. He continued to be impressed by the way Baby was handling her business since the two had been a team. They had come so far in a short period of time, he thought. He reflected on the chain of events. They had been running nonstop. Since the two of them had escaped from the mental institution and become fugitives of justice, it had been one big, chaotic whirlwind. Neither had a chance to breathe. They had every law enforcement officer you could think of looking for them. They simply made do with what they took along the way to survive, doing whatever it took, from robbing to stealing and even killing if they had to. Now, they had money, a car, and a place to lay their heads.

Baby was used to all of that, growing up in a two-parent home, but she knew he wasn't. For the moment, she wanted to pretend that life as they knew it was normal. It had been so long that she was beginning to forget what normal felt like. Being on the run had her on edge and feeling like a hunted animal. It was beginning to take a toll on her. Baby just wanted to get away from all of that so this was perfect.

"*Mi casa es su casa.*" She stood in the doorway smiling. She used her hand to guide Treacherous inside the house.

She knew that this was a new chapter in their lives and needed to be as perfect as it could be under the circumstances. Treacherous accepted her invitation. He entered the home and stepped foot into the living room. He took in the whole 1200-square-foot area of the two-bedroom home. The furniture was a seven-piece, chocolate leather set. A sixty-inch Sharp flat screen complemented the area.

Treacherous made his way into the kitchen. He opened up the fridge. Baby had made sure both it and the freezer were piled up. She had also fully stocked the cabinets with food and beverages as well as color-coordinated dishes and pans. Baby could tell Treacherous was pleased. He walked from room to room taking it all in. She was nervous and happy at the same time as she watched him examine their new home.

Treacherous walked into the bathroom and looked at the two matching Polo towels hanging on the towel rack, and the toothbrushes that sat neatly on the counter. Baby followed. She stopped and posted up in the doorway of the bathroom while he toured the house. She caught a glimpse of her reflection in the mirror. Within recent weeks, her face had a dark and vague look to it, but today she caught herself smiling. It was a vision she thought she could possibly get used to. It made her feel good to make her man feel good. Treacherous brushed past Baby. He gave her an approving nod and flashed her an inviting smile.

Baby followed him back into the bedroom. On the navy blue comforter bed set were a bunch of outfits in bags, and boxes of sneakers and boots, from Air Max to Timberlands, lined the floor. She had gone all out for him. There were True Religion jeans and a few pair of a new popular jean that originated from New Jersey called Red Tags. She had come across them on a commercial late one night on an urban cable station. She had a bundle of tees along with assorted Polo and Lacoste shirts that would have Treacherous looking like a model in a *GQ* magazine. Baby felt like a parent watching her child on Christmas morning as she watched the love of her life. She continued to lean in the doorway of their bedroom, leaning up against the hinges as he skimmed through the clothes. The more he was impressed, the more she was pleased.

"How did you get this place and all of this done so quick?" Treacherous turned toward her.

"Don't concern yourself with those details." She smiled.

The look in his eyes was priceless. For a moment she believed he seemed to be at peace. Her heart fluttered. No one had ever made her feel the way he did. The feeling was so strong it scared her.

He looked at the décor and walked over to the dresser to the array of cologne bottles, from Guilty Gucci to Armani, that were neatly placed there. He looked in the mirror and quickly turned around and looked at her. It was apparent by the way her hand was on her hip and her face was semi-twisted that she was waiting for a response.

"Wow, bae . . ." he began.

"I hope you like, because it's all for you."

"Like it?"

"Yes, Treach. I wanted it to be perfect."

"I love it." Treacherous nodded again. "You did good." Treacherous beamed.

"You are worth every dime."

Treacherous walked over to her. "I love the hell out of you." He wrapped his arms around her.

"I love the hell out of you too," she returned.

Treacherous stared into her eyes. He grinned. Then he pulled her in tighter and kissed her passionately. The kiss was so strong that his tongue nearly slipped down her throat. Baby was caught off guard by the unexpected kiss. But that didn't stop her from embracing it. She was enjoying every bit of it. His tongue explored her mouth and proceeded to wrestle with her tongue. His hands began to glide in between every crevice of her curvaceous body. He cupped her round ass. Her knees weakened. She melted in his arms. His embrace felt like heaven on her body. She felted intoxicated with drunken love although she was sober.

Treacherous broke away from the embrace. He shoved all the clothes off the bed and guided Baby onto it. He removed his shirt and stood there in his jeans looking at her with a seductive look of desire in his eyes. He slithered his way onto the bed. All in one motion, he peeled her out of her black leggings. He peered down at the black sheer thong she wore. He then began to plant light kisses on the inner part of her thighs while sliding up to remove her BeBe tee.

Baby lay there anticipating his next move but enjoying every minute of it. Treacherous had her completely nude. He spread her legs and wrapped his lips around her clit. His tongue danced in a circular motion as he rubbed on her erect nipples. Baby let out mini moans of pleasure as he devoured her. The feeling was so intense. Treacherous placed two of his fingers inside of Baby's wetness. She squirmed in delight. He continued to sex Baby with his fingers. She grew wetter and wetter. Treacherous knew she was ready. He guided his rock-hard dick inside her tight, wet hole. Baby's love box moistened more. She opened her legs wider. Treacherous plunged deeper inside of her with long and hard thrusts. With each thrust she got more excited. The two kissed as he went deeper and deeper inside of her love canal. They made love for hours before finally passing out. They faced each other. Baby lay there with her arms over his back and her legs wrapped around his. Their love juices and perspiration intertwined. Baby reached her hand up and began to stroke the side of his face. He had already started to doze while his semi-erect manhood was still inside of her. She lay there motionless as she watched Treacherous rest. *Job well done,* she thought, right before she too closed her eyes and drifted off.

Chapter Fourteen

Arthur Love hit his blinker and turned into the cheap motel's parking lot. For the past hour or so, he and Randle had been up, down, and all throughout the city, searching for leads that would bring them closer to tracking down Treacherous and Baby. So far they had come up empty-handed.

"Well, this is pretty much the last one in the area," Love announced as he pulled into the Quality Inn & Suites motel on East Cary Street.

"What the hell." Andre Randle tossed his hands up in the air. "We're already here. Might as well."

Arthur Love chuckled as he put the unmarked car in park. They both took a quick survey of the area then made their way to the motel lobby. Arthur Love spilled into the lobby as Andre Randle followed suit. The first thing they noticed was that the front desk was unattended.

"Hello?" Arthur Love called out. He looked from left to right. No one answered or appeared.

"Maybe they're on a lunch break?" Andre Randle paced the lobby.

"This time of day?" Arthur Love looked at his watch.

"Bathroom break?" Andre Randle shrugged. He was all too ready to throw in the towel. He was already convinced they had run into yet another dead end.

Arthur Love's patience grew thinner by the second. He walked over to the counter and frantically rang the guest bell on top of the counter. "Hello, hello, hello," he sang as he looked left to right for a second time. This time, as his eyes shifted, something caught his attention in front of him. When he looked forward, Arthur Love noticed that the motel surveillance monitors were snowy. His reaction caught Andre Randle by surprise, startling him. In a New York minute, Arthur Love had his service-issue weapon drawn. He began waving his gun in all directions, securing the perimeter. By now Andre Randle had his weapon out and cocked. He too waved his gun in all directions, backing Arthur Love up. Arthur Love made his way behind the motel countertop. The body lying up under the counter confirmed what Arthur Love had already suspected.

Arthur Love kneeled down. He checked the body's left wrist for a pulse. "We got a 187." Arthur Love stood up.

Andre Randle couldn't believe it. "You think it's connected?" he asked Arthur Love. He had called this one wrong and was now unsure.

"This was a hit," Arthur Love announced. "Mafia style," he added.

Andre Randle shook his head. "It's a good thing I wasn't a gambling man," Andre Randle confessed.

Andre Randle couldn't believe their bad luck. He also couldn't believe how the bad guys seemed to always stay one step ahead of them.

Chapter Fifteen

Twenty-eight-year-old Carl Davis peered up at the entrance of the store at the sound of its doorbell ringing off, alerting him that he had a customer. He flashed a welcoming smile at the couple who had just stepped foot into the establishment that his elderly father had owned but he had proudly managed for the past six years, seven days a week. No one knew more about motorcycles than Carl, not even his father, let him tell it. Since a young boy, he had learned how the machines worked inside and out. He had built his first motorcycle from the ground up by age thirteen. By the time he was twenty-one he had a degree in engineering and a certification in mechanics. Had it not been for his father having a stroke, Carl Davis would still be in school furthering his education to become a master on bikes. Nonetheless, he couldn't be happier doing what he loved, which was fixing and selling motorcycles.

"Good afternoon, may I help you guys?" he greeted them as he came from behind the counter.

"We're just looking right now," Treacherous announced in a nonchalant manner.

"Okay, no problem. Well, let me know if you guys need any assistance." Carl flashed another customer-friendly smile. Treacherous's demeanor did not faze him one bit. Within the past six years, he had sold bikes to or worked on them for people of all walks of life. He believed if you had a love for bikes, then there was a universal love and respect you had for those who did as well, no matter race, gender, or where you grew up; so he got along with even the hardest of people.

Carl Davis made his way back around the counter. Treacherous and Baby browsed the many rows of bikes inside Davis Motors.

"These bikes are for whites and old people," Baby turned to Treacherous and said. "We need something with more power to make a statement," she added.

Her words carried just enough to catch Carl Davis's attention. He cleared his throat. "Excuse me, not to be in your business, but—"

"But you are." Baby shot him a murderous look.

Carl Davis's eyes widened at Baby's rebuttal. Still he continued from behind the counter. "And I do apologize; it's just that I may have—"

"You may have what, mutha—" Baby snapped with attitude cutting Carl Davis off for a second time. But she too was cut off in midsentence.

"Babe, chill." Treacherous jumped in. He rubbed the back of Baby's arm to calm her. "We not here for all of that," he reminded her in her ear. He swept the establishment visually and saw the video cameras in each corner of the walls. He knew the last thing either of them needed was to cause a scene and draw unnecessary attention to themselves. They had more than enough money now to get what they came for without any incident. They were there for one reason and one reason only: to find two bikes.

Treacherous's words caused Baby to relax. By now, Carl Davis was just mere inches away from Treacherous and Baby. "She's right." He directed his words to Treacherous. "These bikes aren't for you guys. You need something with more style . . . and power!" he added with excitement in his tone. He snapped his fingers to put emphasis on his words.

Baby and Treacherous looked at each other. It took everything in Baby's power to keep from laughing. Instead, she smiled at Treacherous with her eyes. Carl Davis knew he had their attention.

"Follow me." He waved them on as he began to walk toward the back of the store behind a curtain. When Treacherous and Baby entered the back room, their eyes widened. It was as if they had just stepped into motorcycle heaven. Some of the dopest and most powerful bikes in existence lined the walls.

"Welcome," Carl Davis announced. He was used to the reaction Treacherous and Baby had once he revealed his back room to them. Being a white kid who knew about bikes made him accepted by all. He was actually responsible for the majority of the tricked-out bikes that roamed the streets of Virginia. His reputation preceded him and he had received countless referrals by satisfied customers.

"Yeah." Treacherous nodded. He rubbed his hands together. "This is what we need right here."

Baby scanned the room. Her eyes had already zeroed in on a few bikes to choose from.

"What did I tell you, huh?" Carl Davis was in his element. His tone had become more confident. Baby was not feeling his cocky attitude. She was tempted to check him, but sided against it. She knew Treacherous would disapprove. Besides, she couldn't deny it; Carl Davis possessed some great bikes.

"So, what's your choice of drug?" Carl Davis asked. "Suzuki? Yamaha?"

Neither Treacherous nor Baby answered. Instead they made their way over to the bikes that had caught their eye. Carl Davis just watched. Treacherous was the first one to stop next to a bike.

"Ah, yes, great choice!" Carl Davis scurried over to where Treacherous stood. "The Kawasaki Ninja ZX-14R," he announced. "Superlative performance. This is actually the fastest and strongest sports bike in the world!"

Treacherous glanced over at him. That was something he did not know. Carl Davis continued, explaining about the front and rear suspension and the special ABS brakes. He finished by saying, "It's definitely a great twenty-thou-sand-dollar investment."

Hearing the bike's price made Treacherous cut his eyes over at Carl Davis. He was familiar with the terms Carl Davis was using but he was not interested in any of that. He was only concerned about one thing in case of emergency. "How fast does it go?" he asked abruptly.

"Oh, good question." Carl Davis smiled. "This baby has 180 on the dash."

"I didn't ask you what was on the dash; I asked you how fast it can go. Or how fast can you make it go?"

By now, Baby drew her attention over to Treacherous and Carl Davis. A confused look appeared on Carl Davis's face. It took him a second to process what Treacherous was asking him.

"Um, that's not legal." Carl Davis's words came out choppy. "Besides, it's expensive," he added. He took an-other look at Treacherous and then over at Baby. They did not strike him as the type who could afford what Carl Davis believed Treacherous was inquiring about. For the first time, Carl Davis had taken a good look at Treacher-ous and Baby.

"What's your price range? And what does your credit score look like?" he asked in the nicest tone he could con-jure up. He was beginning to regret bringing the couple into the back room without establishing all of that first.

Baby was the first to take offense. "Motherfucker, did we say we were looking to finance something?" she snapped. She bobbed in and out of the rows of bikes making a beeline straight for Carl Davis. He was clueless as to the imminent danger he was faced with but Treacherous knew. Before Baby could reach where they stood, Treacherous pulled out a wad of cash containing nothing but one hundred dollar bills.

"There is no price limit and we prefer cash over credit." Carl Davis's eyes widened. He realized he had literally just judged a book by its cover. *Holy fuck, that's got to be at least fifty grand,* thought Carl Davis.

He was now clear on exactly who and what he was dealing with, so he thought. He never noticed that Baby was just about to draw her gun, intending to send his brain matter flying across the room before they helped themselves to what they had come for. She had released the butt of her pistol when she saw Treacherous pull out the money.

"I understand," Carl Davis retorted. "How about you guys pick the bikes you want, tell me what you need done to them, and you pick them back up first thing in the morning?" Carl Davis flashed his customer-friendly smile once again.

"Nah, we need 'em today," Treacherous corrected him.

Carl Davis thought for a second. He stared out at nothing in particular as if he were searching for an answer. Then just like that, he said, "Okay, later today it is! I'll give you guys some time alone to decide what you want. I'll be up front when you're done," he concluded.

"Cool," Treacherous replied. Baby rolled her eyes. She badly wanted to put a bullet through the cheek of Carl Davis to give him a permanent smile.

"What's up with you?" Treacherous asked as soon as Carl Davis disappeared behind the curtain.

"Nothing!" she replied dryly. "I just don't like that shit-eatin'-grin muthafucker," she confessed. "From the time we walked in he had that same fake-ass smile on his face he been flashin' us."

Treacherous shook his head and chuckled. "That's his job, Baby. Come on, let's pick out these bikes before you catch another body to add to our laundry list."

That made Baby smile. "I already know which one I want," she replied.

"Okay, me too. Let's take care of this and get the fuck out of here."

"My thoughts exactly," Baby agreed.

Chapter Sixteen

Neiko opened the door and found Sammy Black Jr. sitting behind a long brown-marble desk in the office of the Black's family restaurant.

"Long time no see," Sammy Black Jr. greeted Neiko Bellini as he entered his office.

"Yes, it has been, my friend," Neiko Bellini agreed.

Sammy Black Jr. stood and stepped from behind his desk. The two men exchanged hugs and kisses on the cheek. There was a mutual respect between the two men, despite the differences in their career choices, and for good reason.

"You hungry?" Sammy Black Jr. wasted no time asking.

"Sure, I can eat," Neiko Bellini replied.

"Good. Follow me." Sammy Black Jr. instructed. He was really glad to see Bellini. There was no doubt in his mind that with the help of him, he'd soon have those responsible for his father's death in front of him. After all, he had prevailed in the past, many of times. Sammy knew there was no way his family could have been as powerful as they were without the help of their inside law enforcement connect. He was introduced to Neiko Bellini, a half-Irish, half-Italian twenty-year-old, by his father when he was a young teen, fresh out of the academy. Since then, Sammy had linked up with the crooked cop, back when he was just a rookie. With Sammy's help, Neiko took down some of Richmond's biggest crime bosses. The information contributed to the opportunity of their family business expanding.

Twelve years later, the two were still loyal crime part-
ners. Whether he had to sweep something under the rug
to keep Sammy out of the limelight, destroy or manip-
ulate evidence, or take out other competition to keep
Sammy's profits high, Neiko stuck to his word and took
care of it.

The last four years had tested Neiko in a way that he
had never been tested before. He was used to only handling things within the city limits of Richmond for Sammy. But Sammy, on the contrary, was very ambitious
and wanted to branch out more. Neiko's police perks
were truly tested as he found ways to negotiate deals
under the table with other law enforcement officers who
also did business with their city's organized crime. The
dirty cop role was something he had perfected, and if
asked to do so in the future for another heavy hitter in
the underworld, Neiko would jump at the chance.

Sammy and Neiko met each other at a mom-and-pop
diner located in downtown Richmond. It was a small,
private place where a criminal and cop could converse
without being noticed. The fact that it was owned by a
relative of Sammy's made it that much more of a safe
place for the meeting. There wasn't a soul in their family
who hadn't heard what happened to his father. He had
the full support of everybody who was connected to the
Blacks' bloodline. Which is why they had no problem
when Sammy asked to utilize the establishment for his
meeting with Neiko Bellini.

"Sorry I go here so late. There was a meeting at the
department. How's everything?" Neiko said, taking a
seat in the empty chair across from where Sammy sat.
He noticed two of Sammy's henchmen in a booth across
from where they sat. He could spot an Irish gangster a
mile away.

Sammy's response drew his attention back to him. "I
ought to be asking you."

"About the motel clerk." Neiko paused briefly before continuing. "You guys are covered. They don't have any evidence linking anybody to the murder. There were no eyewitnesses to place your cousin or anyone else at the murder scene."

"Good." Sammy nodded. "This is for you, a present." He tapped Neiko on the leg under the table with an envelope containing $10,000. "I'll make sure the rest is in that account before the day is out. Now, let's get down to business."

Neiko took the money and slipped it into his pants pocket. "They do, however"—he cleared his throat—"know that you guys are on those black kids' tail. So, you may get a visit from two of mine."

Sammy Black grimaced. "What the fuck for?" he growled.

"Relax." Neiko Bellini didn't back down. "There's nothing I could do to stop it. This freakin' case is just as personal to them as it is for you," he informed Sammy Black.

"How so?" Sammy wanted to know.

"For starters, the girl is the goddamn daughter of a hot shot black detective."

"Are you fucking shittin' me?" Sammy chuckled. He leaned back and grabbed hold of his head.

"No, wait. It gets better," Neiko Bellini exclaimed. "The other one is the chief of police over in Norfolk."

A confused look appeared across Sammy Black's face. "So, what's his business over here?" he asked.

"Excuse me," the waitress, one of Sammy's younger cousin's, appeared out of nowhere and interjected. "Sorry to bother you cousin Sammy, but aunt Lydia told me to ask you did you and your friend want anything?" Her Irish accent made her words sound rhythmic.

Her eyes shifted from Sammy Black Jr. to Neiko Bellini.

Both men abruptly became silent and drew their attention toward the waitress.

"Bring me a water with lemon and house beer please, sweetie." Sammy smiled.

"And for you sir?" She directed her words to Bellini.

"Just water for me. No lemon."

"Okay, can I start you off with any appetizers?"

"Just tell aunt Lydia to send whatever she feels we'll like," Sammy decided.

He was eager to hear what Neiko had to say.

"Yes, cousin Sammy," she replied as she bowed and made her exit. It didn't take a genius to figure out he wanted privacy.

"As you were saying." Sammy said to Neiko as soon as his little cousin had vanished in the back.

"His business is," Neiko began, "that he killed the mother of the boy; and apparently these fucking niggers broke out of a freakin' crazy hospital, teamed up, and killed the girl's mother and shot both of these two idiots in the process of fleeing." He ended with a sigh.

"Holy Mother of Mary," Sammy chimed.

"Exactly. So that's why I couldn't intervene, because I'd draw suspicion. Suspicion neither one of us needs."

Sammy Black nodded. "You're right. If they come, I'll just curve 'em. Let's discuss more important things, like leads on these two little shits with our fucking money and chips."

"I'm all over it," Neiko assured Sammy. "After the motel info, the trail's been cold."

"Shit!" Sammy cursed. It was imperative that he recover the casino chips. Not only to save face among the other families and prevent a possible war, but also because the blueprint his father had left before his unexpected demise revolved around the casino chips. It was his father's dream to open up a slew of casinos in the Virginia area like Bugsy Siegel had done in Las Vegas, Nevada, and many other gangsters and mobsters had done down in

Atlantic City, New Jersey. His father had recently found some people with the resources to make that dream come true, but first he had to prove that he could operate on a much bigger scale than he had ever before. That's where Sammy Black Jr. came into the picture. Those chips stolen by Treacherous and Baby were the link and root of a gambling monopoly.

He shook his head. "Okay, listen. We're still moving forward with taking over the gambling and coke supply in Glen Allen."

Neiko's eyebrows rose. As if the hassle of having to supervise Sammy's moves in the three other cities wasn't enough, now the man wanted to take on another. "You sure about this?"

"More than ever. I'm ready to do this," Sammy exclaimed.

"But Glen Allen?" asked a skeptical Neiko. He almost knocked over Sammy's mug of coffee as he slammed his fists down on the table.

Sammy eyed Neiko as if he had lost his mind. "Is there a problem?"

"Yeah, there is." Neiko slid his chair closer toward the table. "How the fuck do you expect me to help get you out of something in Glen Allen? I'm confident about a lot of shit, but trying to find a cop gone bad out there is one thing I'm not too sure about." He groaned.

Sammy rolled his eyes and scowled. "Stop ya worryin'. I see you don't know nothin' about Glen Allen. That place is full of crooked cops like you." He couldn't help but remind Neiko of his position. "Besides, I'm already in talks with one: my stepbrother, Charlie Vecky."

Neiko looked up toward the ceiling to think about where he knew that name from. "Former Richmond detective Charles Vecky?" Neiko asked.

"Yeah, he relocated, remember? Well, that's where he went. He's ready when I'm ready. All you have to do is make sure shit goes smoothly out here while I'm gone," Sammy told his cop friend.

"Hold on a second, Sammy. I'm sure somebody controls it already. What makes you think you can just walk in there and become the top dog with ease? The drug dealers who do run that town will ask for your head on a platter."

"You let me worry about that," Sammy dryly replied.

Just then the waitress appeared.

"What's wrong? Sammy asked his cousin.

She stood there looking nervous. "Nothing's wrong." Her word came out choppy.

"I just wanted to know was everything to your liking?

At that moment, Sammy felt bad for making her feel afraid.

"Yes, ma'am." he shot her a smile.

That made her light up. "Aunt Lydia will be pleased to hear."

"Tell her I said compliments to the chef." He told her. "And here." He extended a one-hundred dollar bill. "This is for you, for your quality service. Get you something nice."

You could literally count all thirty-two teeth of Sammy's cousin. "Thank you cousin Sammy." She then spun around and scurried off into the back excitedly.

That was very admirable of you," Neiko remarked. He waited until she was out of earshot then turned back to face Sammy.

"I did that because when I looked into her eyes I saw fear. Fear of me." He pointed out to Neiko. "I don't want my family, especially those coming behind me, to fear me, I want them to respect me." He added.

Neiko nodded. He understood Sammy's logic.

"Look, I don't think you have to take this route, but if you're set on it why not try your hand at another city? Take a trip and see what kind of feel you get." He changed subjects.

"What do you suggest?" Sammy was curious to hear his thoughts.

"Well, for starters, it might be easier for a powerful guy like you to blow up right away in one of the seven cities versus Glen Allen, maybe even Williamsburg or Fredericksburg. Let's be logical here. Hell, maybe even in Newport News right across the water."

Sammy waited until Neiko was done. "In everything I do, I am logical. But I hear where you're coming from. I'll look into it," Sammy abruptly ended and stood up.

Neiko knew he couldn't change Sammy's mind. If that man wanted to do something, he'd do it, he told himself. All Neiko could do was offer his bit of advice and hope that Sammy would find it useful.

Neiko pushed his chair back and stood. He stuck his hand in his pocket and pulled out his money clip. He peeled a fifty dollar bill from under the clip and placed it on the table as an additional tip. Sammy's logic had prompted him to leave it. He was touched by it.

Sammy made a beeline for the exit. Neiko followed. He noticed the two henchmen rise up, and he put a little pep in his step. He trailed a close distance as Sammy Black passed through the tables and booths, until they reached the exit. They stepped out into the Virginia summer heat.

"Pleasure as always and thanks." Neiko extended his hand. The two men shook hands. Sammy tightened his grip.

"I need more information on these two pricks fast, Neiko." Sammy stared Neiko Bellini in the eyes. "There's a lot at stake," he added.

Neiko Bellini could see the rage mixed with despair in Sammy Black Jr.'s eyes. He had never before seen him look the way he did at that moment. For the first time, Neiko Bellini wondered the actual value of what Treacherous Freeman and Baby Love had stolen from the Blacks' pawnshop.

"Don't worry. I'm on it." Neiko Bellini tightened his grip to match Sammy Black's. "If they're in the state of Virginia, I'll find them," he boldly stated. "Even if I have to get out there and track them down myself," he added.

Chapter Seventeen

Treacherous watched as male and female bodies passed by where he and Baby sat in the car. Tonight they chose to leave their bikes parked.

"You sure you want to try to get in?" he asked for the umpteenth time. In all honesty, he was actually the one who was not so sure. Crowds were not his thing and neither was the club scene. He had never been to one and didn't have the desire to go. It was Baby's idea. She had come up with an entire plan on how they would enjoy what time they had left on the streets.

They had been lying low ever since they had moved into their own place, but Baby felt like she was suffocating. Being in the mental institution had done something to her. She insisted they get out and enjoy some of their newfound riches in their home state before they up and disappeared from Virginia for a little while. She believed the club would be the last place they looked for her and Treacherous, considering they were not legally old enough to get into any of the top establishments. Baby knew that money talked in VA, so she was hoping it talked their way up into the hot spot that seemed to be full throttle already.

Treacherous and Baby observed from afar the flow of operation of the club. They saw how security controlled the two separate lines while club promoters checked groups off their lists and escorted them inside the hot spot. Assorted luxury vehicles and bikes continued to pull in and parked in the parking lot. Treacherous caught the name CHANGE LANE on the backs of the vests of bikers as the social club cruised in. The drivers of a half dozen bikes pulled over and parked beside them while the rest created their own parking spaces. The passengers hopped off the back of the bikes. Treacherous and Baby watched as the group of bikers mobbed together and ignored the long lines in front of the club. They walked straight to the entrance. The huge security guard acknowledged them and unhooked the velvet rope from the brass rail, while stepping to the side. Another guard in a full three-piece suit appeared from out of nowhere and escorted them inside.

Treacherous's and Baby's attention was drawn to the females in packs with next to nothing on, strutting past. Most of them were applying lip gloss to their lips and spraying themselves down with their favorite fragrances, while dudes in cliques floated past rotating blunts, Black & Milds, and unfinished bottles of liquor before they reached the front entrance of the club. Treacherous and Baby exited the car. The weather couldn't have been more perfect that night. A light, warm breeze filled the air to complement the eighty-four-degree weather Virginia Beach was having.

Club Aqua in Virginia Beach off of Virginia Beach Boulevard was one of the places to be on the weekend. The old Virginia House of Comedy's Friday and Saturday nights were guaranteed to be jumping. Partygoers from all over came in droves to turn up at the nightclub. The storefront-style club's blue AQUA neon sign illuminated the top of the establishment. Treacherous and Baby rolled up to the front of the club. They both looked to the left and right of them. The VIP entrance on their left flowed steadily while the general admission line on their right moved at a snail's pace. Treacherous noticed someone staring at him. It was one of the club promoters with a clipboard in his hand. Treacherous matched the man's stare as he started making a beeline over toward him and Baby.

"Y'all got a table or on a list?" the club promoter asked abruptly.

Treacherous shot him a blank stare. "Nah," Treacherous dryly replied.

"Is everything okay, Gov?" one of the bouncers chimed in. He and Treacherous were nearly matched in height and build. That still didn't stop Treacherous from directing his attention to the man and shooting him a rock stare. The bouncer instantly caught it.

"Is there a problem?" The bouncer stared into Treacherous's eyes.

"Not unless you causing one," Treacherous retorted.

Baby was tempted to intervene, but she knew Treacherous could handle the situation. In her mind, she was already contemplating running back to the car and grabbing her and Treacherous's guns if shit hit the fan outside the club.

"He good, Big Junior, I got him," the club promoter referred to as Gov interjected on Treacherous's behalf. The club was rocking too much to have it shut down over a frivolous pissing contest, thought Gov.

"Step over here with me." Gov directed his words to Treacherous and Baby. "I can get y'all straight in if y'all doing bottle service," he wasted no time informing them.

"Okay," Baby answered for the both of them.

"Cool." Gov smiled. "They call me the Ghetto Governor and I'll be taking care of you," he chimed.

The sound of his name resonated in Treacherous's mind. For some reason, he thought he had heard the name Ghetto Governor before, but couldn't place it.

"I just need to know what package you want, two bottle minimum for where I'd like to put y'all," he announced.

"That's fine." Baby nodded.

"Big man, that's cool with you?" Ghetto Governor tried to ease what little tension there may have been brewing between Treacherous and the bouncer Big Junior.

"If she's fine with it, so am I." Treacherous's words were straight and to the point.

"No doubt!" Ghetto Governor left it at that. "So, all I need is a credit card and your IDs."

Treacherous and Baby both looked at each other and then back at him. "We're paying cash and . . ." Baby paused. "We don't have any ID on us."

Ghetto Governor scratched his head and grimaced. The cash part was cool, but the no ID was a problem. He stared at the young couple long and hard. They each appeared to be twenty-one or older to him. He had pulled strings in the past for others from the hood to famous celebrities, but they were neither of the two, he thought. Ghetto Governor pondered it for a few more seconds and then said, "It's gonna cost you an extra two hundred each for the no ID."

Treacherous let out an insane chuckle. Before he could deliver the words he intended to spew at Ghetto Governor, Baby replied, "No problem." She had already pulled out the monstrous knot she had in her jeans pocket. "What's the total?"

"Whoa!" Ghetto Governor's eyes grew as they zeroed in on the wad of cash. He estimated the money to be $10,000 or more. *Maybe they are somebody,* he thought. *They can't be from the seven cities and I don't know them.* Seeing the money piqued his interest in wanting to find out about the couple though.

"We'll take care of all of that inside," he explained. "Put your money away. Right now, I just need your names for the list."

"Treacherous," Treach was first to announce. Baby followed up with her name, but her words fell on deaf ears. Ghetto Governor was still trying to process the first name given by Treacherous.

Naw. It can't be, Ghetto Governor reasoned with himself. *It must be a coincidence.* Ghetto Governor cleared his throat. "Young brother, I got a question to ask." He paused. "And I mean no disrespect, but what's your parents' names?"

The question came out of nowhere, surprising both Treacherous and Baby. Treacherous's first instinct was to grab the club promoter by the throat and choke the life out of him, but something in Ghetto Governor's tone made him believe that there was no malice behind his question. Baby stood on guard awaiting Treacherous's reaction so that she could follow suit.

Treacherous looked Ghetto Governor up and down. "Why you wanna know that?" Treacherous asked. His demeanor was stoic.

Ghetto Governor could understand Treacherous's apprehensive and defensive demeanor. If the roles were reversed, he knew he would react the same way. He was convinced there was no coincidence in the names. Nor was it a coincidence that Treacherous acted the same way. "Man, if your mom's and pop's names are Treacherous and Teflon then we damn near like family!" Ghetto Governor chimed.

The mention of his parents' names woke something up inside of Treacherous. It was the first time he had ever met anyone who knew them. For this stranger to be claiming to know them piqued his interest. The club promoter's name resonated in Treacherous's mind. It now dawned on him where he had heard the name Ghetto Governor before. His mother had mentioned the club promoter in her journals. Treacherous knew his mother's journals practically by heart. Which was why it was easy for him to quickly reflect on why Ghetto Governor's name was mentioned. Outside of helping his parents out with some valuable information, there was nothing that would indicate that Ghetto Governor was like family, thought Treacherous.

Still, Treacherous had a newfound respect for Ghetto Governor now that he was familiar with his name. Once upon a time, he had helped his parents and for that Treacherous felt the club promoter deserved to be shown some respect. Treacherous extended his hand. Ghetto Governor embraced it.

"Appreciate what you did for them," Treacherous offered with a firm grip.

His words caught Ghetto Governor by surprise. *How could he know?* he wondered. He knew he wasn't old enough to have known that. *He wasn't even a thought back then,* he continued, realizing Treacherous couldn't have even been born. He could tell Treacherous knew though. Ghetto Governor nodded. "No doubt, black man," he accepted. "Let me get y'all set up in here, so y'all can enjoy the rest of your evening," Ghetto Governor then bellowed. "Yeah, I'ma set y'all up real nice," he added admirably.

Treacherous and Baby followed as Ghetto Governor led the way. "Jayski, they're with me," he informed his management team partner as Big Junior unhooked the velvet rope.

It wasn't even midnight and Club Aqua was nearly at its maximum capacity of a thousand heads. DJ Jack Of Spade of 103 Jamz had the club turned up. Baby's hips swayed to the sound of Drake's voice while Treacherous scanned the hot spot as Ghetto Governor continued to lead the way.

"Shout out to the Jolly Brothers," DJ Jack Of Spade boomed into the microphone. "They just got signed to Cash Money," he announced. "And shout out to my mans Corte Ellis and DJ Boo, I see y'all baby!" he added. Just then, Rick Ross's infamous grunt came blaring out of the speakers.

The energy in the club was ridiculous. After passing other VIP sections, Ghetto Governor stopped in front of the section he intended to set Treacherous and Baby up in. The section was perfect, thought Baby. It was in the heart of the club, with a replica next to it. The U-shaped leather sectional was just what Baby had in mind.

"The server will be with you in a minute," Ghetto Governor bellowed over the music.

Just then, a *Soul Train* line of sexy bottle servers trailing behind one another, with assorted bottles of liquor held high in the air, appeared out of nowhere. Sparklers illuminated the club as the six sexy women delivered a dozen bottles to the section right next to theirs. The section was overflowing with gorgeous women of all shades and dudes who appeared to be body builders, aside from one man in an expensive-looking suit who would remind you of the actor Joe Pesci.

"Shout out to all my bottle poppers," DJ Jack of Spade screamed into the mic. "Dexter Reid, showin' that NFL love," he added, referring to the ex–New England Patriot and two-time Super Bowl champion, who was responsible for the train of bottles the servers bought to the table next to Treacherous and Baby. Dexter Reid raised his fist up in the air toward the DJ booth.

"That's the owner, Steve." Ghetto Governor pointed out the man in the expensive-looking suit to Treacherous and Baby. "I'm gonna go check on your server and then head back out. I got work to do," he informed them.

Baby pulled out a few hundreds. "Don't forget the extra money for the IDs," she reminded him.

"Naw, y'all straight." He waved the money off. He refused to accept the extra money he intended to charge them for not having any identification. It just didn't feel right to him, knowing who Treacherous's parents were and what they had done for him. It was because of them that Ghetto Governor had enough money to pay off his home and put a nice chunk of money up for his kids' college tuition. Ghetto Governor reflected on the last time he had seen Treacherous and Teflon. After the caper they had pulled off that he had put them down on, they had dropped off a knapsack to Ghetto Governor with nearly two hundred grand inside.

"Like I said before, you like family." Ghetto Governor returned to the present. He reached into the inside of his suit jacket. "Take this." He handed Treacherous his business card. "If you ever need anything, I mean anything," he emphasized, "don't hesitate to call me." Seconds later, Ghetto Governor vanished into the crowd.

Treacherous pulled out his wallet and slipped the business card into it. He had gotten a good feeling about Ghetto Governor. He believed his words to be genuine and sincere.

Moments later, Treacherous and Baby's server appeared. She was beyond beautiful. They both noticed the girl's breasts protruding from the top of her tee, and her cleavage glistened.

"Hello, my name is Monae and I'll be your server." The curvaceous server with a Hershey Bar complexion beamed with a smile.

Treacherous and Baby both nodded.

"So, you guys know what you'd like?" Monae the server directed her attention to Treacherous.

Treacherous pointed and directed her to Baby. This was all new to him. Neither of them were drinkers, but Baby was familiar with liquors. Most of her family drank, from young to old.

"Bring us a bottle of 1738 and bottle of peach Cîroc." Baby ordered a bottle of Rémy and P. Diddy's popular vodka.

Monae the server jotted down the order as Baby spoke. "What chasers would you like?"

Baby spit out three chasers for the liquor as if she were a veteran at ordering bottles.

"Okay, I'll be right back." Monae the server smiled and exited.

Treacherous nodded his head to the sounds of Troy Ave's latest track while he observed those in the club. The dance floor was infested with bodies all shapes, sizes, and colors. Dudes were doing their best two-steps, while chicks broke out in twerk positions.

"Yes, I needed this!" Baby chimed. Treacherous peered over at her. She was now dancing where she sat. The song had switched to 50 Cent's "In Da Club." Just then, Monae the server reappeared with three chasers consisting of ginger ale, and cranberry and orange juice, along with a white receipt dangling from her hand.

"I'll take that," Baby yelled over the music in regard to the bill. Monae the server smiled.

"Nah, I got it, bae," Treacherous interjected before Monae could hand Baby the bill. He had already pulled his knot of cash out. Monae's eyes lit up at the sight of the money. Baby noticed the sudden change in the server.

"Here you go, sir." She flashed Treacherous a huge smile. She inconspicuously scanned Treacherous up and down. Everything about him checked out, she thought. She noticed he was draped in designer gear from head to toe. Monae had a nose for money and she was beginning to suffocate from the smell oozing off of Treacherous. Normally she could tell by a guy's accessories, but he didn't rock any jewelry. His wardrobe was enough for her though. It matched his monstrous knot she was still eyeing.

The receipt came to just under $700. Treacherous pulled eight hundred-dollar bills from his bankroll and handed them to Monae the server. In her mind she had counted with him, already smiling from what she believed would be her gratuity.

"Don't worry about the change," Treacherous announced.

"Thank you." Monae beamed. Her eyes became seductive as she stared at Treacherous too long for Baby's taste.

"How long before our bottles come?" Baby chimed in, breaking Monae out of her temporary trance.

"Any minute now." She turned to Baby and flashed her a warm smile. Baby returned her smile with a cold, blank stare. She was not feeling the server. She had caught how her demeanor had changed when Treacherous pulled out his money. *Gold-digging bitch,* Baby thought. She was tempted to put Monae in her place but didn't want to mess up the good energy she was enjoying being in the club. Monae must have picked up on Baby's vibe, because she excused herself abruptly. Within minutes, she was parading through the crowd with Treacherous and Baby's two bottles, while a buff brother carrying a metal bucket of ice accompanied her.

The sparklers guided her to where they sat. "What would you guys like to drink?" Monae asked. Her eyes shifted from Treacherous to Baby, but her attention was more so directed toward Treacherous.

"We got it from here, boo boo, thanks." Baby grabbed Monae's wrist lightly, preventing her from scooping the ice out of the bucket to prepare them drinks.

"Oh okay." Monae was thrown back. "Let me know if you need anything else. I'll be back to check on you." She hit Baby with her customer-friendly smile for a second time.

Baby said nothing. She just continued to stare at Monae. Treacherous nodded and flashed a half of a grin.

Monae turned and made her exit. "Bitch," she mumbled under her breath out of earshot of Baby.

Baby shook her head as soon as she walked off. Treacherous laughed. "What?"

"That stupid-ass server, that's what," Baby replied. "I'm trying to have a good time, but this disrespectful bitch trying to bring me out of character." Baby rolled her eyes.

"Ain't nobody thinking about her," Treacherous assured Baby.

"I know, but it doesn't mean she not thinking about you, with her money-hungry ass," Baby spat.

Treacherous chuckled. "Yeah, I saw her eyes almost pop out her head."

"Yeah, well, you almost seen me rip them shits out of her head," Baby snapped back.

"Fuck her, let's enjoy this night while we can." Treacherous became serious. "Pour me a drink since you ran our server off."

Baby smiled. "Yes, sir," she mocked Monae the server. Baby poured Treacherous a double shot of 1738 with no ice and herself a double shot of Cîroc on the rocks. She handed Treacherous the glass.

"To us!" Baby toasted. "Ride or die!" she ended. Just then, the Jay-Z and Beyoncé "Bonnie & Clyde" track filled the room. Baby tossed her drink back and then hopped up from where she sat. She began to become one with the music.

Treacherous leaned back sipping on the strong drink while he watched as Baby's body moved in a snake form.

With each motion Treacherous got turned on more and more. He downed the remainder of the cognac then leaned forward and poured them both another drink. Baby took the drink, the whole while never missing a beat as Beyoncé's melodic voice was replaced with Rihanna's bad girl sound.

Treacherous watched with lustful eyes as Baby's hips swayed from left to right. She flashed him a smile that reminded him of the reason why he loved her so much. He took a swig of his drink then leaned back for a second time. At that moment, Treacherous was having a great time. Not because he was underage in a club in VIP with bottles, but because the woman he loved appeared to be having the time of her life. He hadn't seen Baby that happy since he'd known her. He wished it could stay the way it was right then and there forever but he knew that was an unrealistic wish. Treacherous shook off his thoughts and decided to focus on that moment. For the next hour Treacherous sat tossing drinks back while watching Baby as she danced and did the same with her drinks. The liquor had begun to take effect on the both of them.

"I gotta use the ladies' room." Baby leaned over in Treacherous's direction. Her words were somewhat slurred, but Treacherous didn't pick up on it due to the loud music.

"You want me to come with you?" Treacherous was about to stand but Baby stopped him.

"I'm good. I'm a big girl." She smiled. "I'll be right back.

Treacherous studied her. "A'ight."

Baby spun around. She looked up and located the nearest EXIT sign lit up on the wall then made her way through the crowd. She knew wherever an exit sign was a bathroom was not too far away.

***

Moments later Baby exited the ladies' room. Her head was spinning like a carousel. She didn't realize she was as drunk as she actually was. Her vision was blurry from the Cîroc. She regretted not taking Treacherous up on his offer to escort her to the bathroom as she struggled to locate their VIP section.

"You good, ma?" a tall, dark-skinned brother walking past with cornrows and a goatee asked Baby.

"Get the fuck outta here." Baby waved him off without bothering to look in the tall, dark-skinned brother's direction.

The brother chuckled and kept walking.

Baby could have sworn he called her a drunk bitch. She wished she had gotten a look at his face for when the club was over. Baby grabbed hold of her forehead. *Get your shit together,* she told herself. She couldn't focus. She shook her head and wiped her face. Her vision seemed to be a little clearer than before but the club's lights didn't help any. Baby knew she had come from the right side of the club. She scanned the sections until she noticed something familiar. She wasted no time making a beeline, weaving in and out of the club-goers, in the direction she believed her and Treacherous's section was.

Minutes later, she was standing in the perfect position to execute what she had envisioned herself doing once she got back across the club. Before Treacherous or anybody else knew what was happening, Baby had already landed her first punch. The right straight jab to the side of Monae the server's face was not strong enough to knock her out because Baby was liquored up. It was, however, effective enough to daze her. Before Monae could recover from the blow, Baby had already followed up with a left hook that sent her flying on top of the remainder of her bottle of Cîroc.

By now, the attention of those within short distance of the commotion was drawn to Treacherous and Baby's VIP section. The nearest bouncer had already radioed in the incident as he made his way over to where the altercation was. Treacherous sobered up immediately as soon as he saw Baby delivering her second punch to Monae's face, who was unsuccessful in her attempt to dodge the blow. He was now on his feet and by Baby's side. He peeped the bouncer headed in their direction. He couldn't do anything but shake his head as he got into battle mode. He felt his anger rising and his rage boiling. He wasn't mad at Baby though. He already had a bad feeling ever since Monae came over and struck up a conversation with him while Baby was in the bathroom. He knew she was flirting with him each time she bent over pretending to clean up the area or wipe something up while she asked random questions. Monae was now curled up on the VIP seat in a fetal position as Treacherous stood in between her and Baby. In a New York minute, eight cock diesel bouncers swarmed Treacherous and Baby's VIP section like killer bees. They all sported black leather gloves and wore black tees two sizes too small for them.

"Let's go!" one of the bouncers barked in Treacherous's direction. He gritted his teeth while eyeing Treacherous down.

"Yeah, a'ight, hold up," Treacherous dryly replied. He turned his back on the bouncer. "Let's get—" Treacherous attempted to tell Baby they needed to leave, but the hand on his shoulder caused him to pause his words.

"Don't fuckin' put ya hands on me!" He shrugged the bouncer's hand off of his shoulder and spun around.

Baby had already gotten into a fighting stance. She too had now sobered up. The other seven bouncers immediately sprang into action. They all moved forward in an attempt to take Treacherous and Baby down from all angles.

"Hold! Hold! Hold!" were the words that stopped everybody in their tracks.

Ghetto Governor parted the bouncers like the Red Sea until he stood in front of Treacherous and Baby. He spread his arms to guard them. "These my folks right here!" he chimed. "I got this."

The bouncers didn't like it, but they all respected Ghetto Governor. "Just get 'em the hell outta here," the head bouncer commanded.

Treacherous shot him a rock stare. His adrenaline was pumping. He wanted nothing more than to break the head bouncer's jaw for talking so tough. He sided against it though out of respect for Ghetto Governor. He knew had Ghetto Governor not shown up, the bouncers would have been all over him and Baby and things would have gotten real ugly.

"I got 'em," Ghetto Governor assured the head bouncer. He then turned to Treacherous and Baby and said, "I gotta get y'all up out of here."

Neither Treacherous nor Baby contested this.

The bouncers parted once again as Ghetto Governor escorted Treacherous and Baby out of the club. Monae the server didn't get up from where she lay until she was sure Treacherous and Baby had exited the club.

Ghetto Governor sighed. "Damn, y'all put me in a crazy position," he confessed.

"Listen, we appreciate you steppin' in and steppin' up, but we could've handled whatever came behind my girl's actions," Treacherous boomed. He was feeling confrontational but was going to honor his initial decision. Still, he wanted Ghetto Governor to know how serious things really could've gotten. "On the strength of you, we're not going to wait until the club closes and do every one of those bouncers dirty."

Ghetto Governor knew Treacherous was serious. *He's definitely Treacherous and Teflon's kid,* thought Ghetto Governor.

"Well, I appreciate that," Ghetto Governor returned. There was a brief silence for a few seconds.

Treacherous was the first to break the ice. "We gonna get out of here." He extended his hand in Ghetto Governor's direction. "Thanks for showing us a boss time."

Ghetto Governor embraced it. He could feel the mini stack of bills touching his palm. This time he accepted the money. He gripped it and shoved it in his pocket. "Don't forget, if you ever need anything, don't hesitate to reach out," Ghetto Governor reminded them.

"I won't." Treacherous nodded. He checked the time on his watch. It was just approaching two a.m.

By two-thirty, he and Baby were cuddled up underneath each other, stealing a few hours before they hopped on the road headed to their next excursion.

Chapter Eighteen

The next day . . .

Baby trailed behind Treacherous's smoke black Ninja on her purple and chrome R1, as they cruised the South Beach area of Miami on their new bikes. Ever since she was a little girl Baby always felt the most freedom when a motorcycle was between her legs and there was endless open road to ride on. She felt as if she hadn't a care in the world at that moment. Getting out of Virginia was just what the doctor had ordered, she thought. They had driven down to Florida, with bikes in tow, putting over 800 miles of distance between themselves and VA.

Baby felt as if she couldn't breathe back home with all that was going on. She never imagined her life would be the way it was presently. She envisioned going off to college to study law and enroll in law enforcement like her dad. She envisioned marrying her high school sweetheart and building a family. Now, here it was: she was fugitive from justice on the other side of the law. Florida made her feel like all of her problems were light years away. The blistering heat put her at peace. It was a different type of heat from Virginia's. She had been comparing the two states ever since they had arrived in Miami three days ago. Each day was more beautiful than the next. This particular sunny day had outdone the rest, thought Baby. The sky was a perfect shade of blue and there were little to no clouds in the sky. Treacherous navigated through the crowded streets. Black Bike Week was in full effect. Normally the two would stay shy of crowds, but with distance between them and Virginia they thought this to be the perfect place for them to get lost in.

The streets and sidewalks were infested with half-naked women of all shades sporting big hats and glasses, and topless males accessorized in jewelry. Baby nearly slammed into the back of Treacherous, who had stopped at the traffic light. Her attention was drawn to a woman standing on the corner next to a bike. She was breathtaking, thought Baby. She had a natural beauty about herself. Her black leather construction boots fit around her ankles perfectly. She had on a pair of jeans that hugged every curve in all the right places. The white tank top accented her breasts and made them look that much more appealing; there was just enough cleavage. Her honey blond tresses fell on her shoulders as she took her helmet off.

Baby found herself mesmerized by her beauty. She couldn't believe she was feeling the way she was. Guilt, shame, and excitement battled within her. She had never thought about anyone but Treacherous but for that minute she had a weakness and it was a feeling that she could not describe. Was she cheating because she thought the stranger was attractive? She began to wonder what it would be like to be with this female willingly as opposed to what she had been exposed to in her childhood.

So consumed was she by her thoughts she had not even realized Treacherous was now right next to her. Sensing that her mind was elsewhere, he broke the silence.

"What's wrong, Baby?" he asked as he took a look at his surroundings.

"Nothing, why you ask?" she replied.

"So you lying now huh?" he asked.

"I saw someone, a female." She paused. "And it gave me a feeling that I've only had for you, sexually," she confessed.

"Where she at?" he asked.

"At the corner, when we stopped," she replied. Baby did not know if she should simply come clean or downplay the situation. She knew Treacherous all too well, so she could not lie or try to conceal what she was truly feeling since they had an open relationship. There were no secrets or lies and he was her true ride or die. "There was something about her that intrigued me." She began to speak in a soft tone.

"So what you want to do?" he asked.

"What?" she shrieked.

"You heard me," he replied.

"Nothing," she said.

"Okay, let's go."

Moments later they were back at their room.

"Tell me, what had you thinking about her?" he asked.

"You really wanna do this?" Baby shot Treacherous a look.

"Yeah, I do."

Baby rolled her eyes. "Okay, she had this natural beauty that had me curious. She had on these denim jeans that were like a second skin and her titties sat perfect in that white wife beater." She spoke with reluctance. "Her hair just sat perfectly on her shoulders and her smile was alluring," Baby said with a partial smile. She peered over at Treacherous. He had a blank stare on his face.

Baby felt uncomfortable with the conversation and no longer wanted to discuss it. She abruptly changed the subject as she began looking for clothes to change into after her shower. Treacherous knew Baby all too well. He couldn't imagine what she was going through inside but he wanted to help her work through whatever it was she was feeling. If she needed to make a decision about her sexuality, then he was not going to stand in her way of deciding.

Baby used the silence as her cue to exit the room and shower. She suddenly felt dizzy and just wanted to simply relax and lie down.

"Baby, I forgot to get some orange juice," Treacherous said breaking the silence.

"Oh, okay. I am going to take a shower and then get into bed," she called out.

Baby entered the bathroom and turned the water on. She grabbed her washcloth. The shower water hitting her face made her feel rejuvenated. It was almost as if the water was cleansing her. Baby felt as if the curious thoughts she had earlier had rinsed off of her and swirled down the drain. She felt a little guilty that she had only revealed a portion of what she was truly thinking about the mystery biker girl to Treacherous.

Baby turned the shower off and reached for her towel. She dried herself and slipped into a pair of boy shorts and put on a bra. She lay across the bed and dozed off for what seemed like hours.

Something broke her sleep. Out of nowhere Baby's eyes shot open and she sprang up. She was speechless when she awakened to a female lying beside her. Thinking it was a dream Baby kept looking at the woman. Once she realized it wasn't she reacted.

"Bitch!" Baby boomed. She instinctively reached under her pillow to retrieve her .380. Surprisingly, it was not there.

"Relax, sexy." The mystery female smiled.

Baby ignored the female's words. Instead, she went into attack mode. The mystery woman was able to hop off the bed just in time to evade Baby's attempted assault.

"Feisty; I like that," the mystery female cooed.

"Who the fuck are you?" Baby bellowed.

"Ask him." The mystery female pointed to the left of them, with a sinister grin plastered across her face.

Baby had no idea Treacherous was in the room the entire time, sitting in the corner. He flashed Baby a smile. Baby shot him daggers.

"Who the fuck is this, Treach?" she demanded to know.

"You don't recognize her?"

"No, should I?" Baby snapped.

"Baby, this is Tammy and she will be joining us tonight."

"Ummm, joining us for what?" Baby questioned.

"This is who you saw at the light," Treacherous refreshed her memory.

Baby took a good look at her. She was gorgeous. Her ass was round and succulent and her breasts were just as inviting. That familiar feeling resurfaced inside of Baby, the one she had gotten early when she first noticed the biker chick. She looked at the mystery female. Before Baby could get a question out, Tammy interrupted.

"Don't worry. I won't hurt neither of you," she said as she winked at the couple.

Tammy got up from the chair she was sitting in and walked over to Baby and immediately started to kiss her. At first Baby was reluctant and made an attempt to resist because she was afraid of what Treacherous would think. Tammy continued to force her tongue in Baby's mouth. But Treacherous shocked her. She felt him behind her grabbing her ass while trying to undress her. That made Baby embrace Tammy's tongue.

Baby's hands began to explore Tammy's voluptuous body. Tammy began to kiss Baby's cheek and neck. Treacherous was pressed up against Baby from behind. She could feel his hardened manhood. He slowly began to grind on her ass. He unbuckled his belt to remove his pants. Baby was nervous. Tammy immediately picked up on it. She handed Baby a glass with pink liquid inside. Baby smelled the fruit aroma and then immediately took a big gulp. Feeling the liquid courage she just consumed, Baby walked up to Tammy and just looked at her body in awe. Then she reached for her waist and brought her closer. So close, she could feel her heartbeat.

The drink took an immediate effect on Baby. Now feeling bold, Baby instructed Tammy to remove her lingerie. She wrapped her arms around Tammy's warm body and pulled her close so that her breasts were touching her skin. For a split second Baby began to doubt herself. Tammy sensed it. She took Baby's hand and rubbed her clit with it, then placed her moist fingers in Baby's mouth. "Don't worry," Tammy said softly. "I'm the one here to please you, so the work is all on me tonight." She winked.

Tammy moved in toward her and began to kiss Baby's neck. It felt electrifying as she teased Baby's flesh with her tongue. She nibbled on her cheeks as she made her way to Baby's lips. She placed soft and delicate pecks on them that made Baby more aroused. Tammy then entered Baby's mouth with her tongue as Treacherous joined in and began to finger Baby's throbbing love cave. Everything felt great. Baby didn't want the feeling to end.

Tammy led Baby to the bed and ordered her to lie on her back. Treacherous began to kiss on Baby's neck and breasts. Tammy moved closer and began to feed Baby her breasts. Her nipples were hard. Baby sucked them like a newborn child. Baby could sense this was sending an electric surge to her pussy. She began to touch herself. Treacherous was turned on by how turned on Baby was. He wanted to continue but knew this was about Baby and not himself. He exited the picture and made his way back over to where he was initially sitting. He groped his hard length and watched as Baby and Tammy explored one another.

After many minutes of watching and fantasizing, Treacherous rejoined the pleasure fest that was taking place in front of him. He pushed Tammy's head in between Baby's legs while pointing his rock-hard dick in Baby's face. Without hesitation Baby firmly sealed her mouth around him. Treacherous loved when Baby made sounds as she sucked on his dick. Baby multitasked by rubbing his sack with her hands and teasing his balls with her tongue, while she slowly ran it from the bottom to the tip then back down to the shaft. After a while Baby just let Treacherous sex her mouth.

Meanwhile, Tammy was feasting between Baby's inner thighs. This was pure bliss for Baby. Tammy began to finger fuck Baby as she sucked on her clit. Tammy steadily moaned as if she was on the receiving end. That just turned Baby on more. She raised her head and winked, while making her way to her mouth. Tammy interrupted the oral sex Baby was performing on Treacherous to kiss her. Baby embraced Tammy's lip lock, then, without warning, Tammy broke free of their tongue lashing and proceeded to lick Treacherous's balls as Baby resumed licking his shaft. Treacherous moaned and groaned in ecstasy.

Tammy moaned, "Hmmmmmm," as she took Treacherous's dick completely inside her mouth. Baby and Tammy took turns performing head on Treacherous's thick length.

Baby looked up at Treacherous. "I want you inside of me," she cooed.

Treacherous did not have to be told twice. He moved Tammy to the side. He lifted Baby up and gently laid her across the bed. Baby parted her legs. She curled her pointer finger and invited Treacherous in. Treacherous positioned himself between her legs and guided his dick inside of Baby's wet box. His rhythm started out with long and slow strokes. Tammy lay there watching. He then started to pick up the pace. Treacherous began to sex Baby faster and harder. Baby was half moaning and whimpering. She closed her eyes as she took his dick. Each stroke was better than the last. When she opened her eyes, this gave way to a clear view of Tammy's perfect pussy. It was neatly shaven with a cherry tattoo on her bikini line. In her curiosity, Baby wanted to taste Tammy. Baby began to softly lick her lips with the tip of her tongue.

Tammy arched her back, which exposed her erect nipples. Treacherous was now sexing Baby from behind. Baby tried her best to sink her tongue deeper into Tammy's pussy, but some of Treacherous's thrusts were making it difficult. She wondered if what she was doing felt to Tammy what it felt like to her when Treacherous was going down on her. Tammy's sex was so wet but it didn't stop Baby from sopping up her juices like she hadn't eaten in days. Baby slid her two fingers inside of Tammy. She let out a long and loud moan.

Baby pleased Tammy's pussy for a couple more minutes before motioning for her to switch positions with her. Without hesitation she stood up. Baby pulled the suction cup release Treacherous had on her loose and stood straight up to stretch.

"I can't be selfish," Baby said.

Tammy didn't need any instructions. Baby could just tell by the look in her pretty brown eyes. "Sit down," she commanded Treacherous. Tammy proceeded to walk in his direction. He immediately grabbed her by her waist then guided her down to his rock-hard dick. Tammy stared into Treacherous's face as she slowly slid the lips of her pretty pussy onto the thick head of his cock. You could see that she was reluctant because of Baby's presence. It was one thing to let another woman give your man head and watch, but fucking was a different story, she believed.

She could tell Baby and Treacherous were young and madly in love. She couldn't figure out why they decided to take a walk on the wild side, but after feeling Treacherous's dick inside of her she didn't care. He felt like a python slithering up and deep into her cave. Tammy bit her bottom lip while focusing on bringing herself down on Treacherous. Inch by inch, she brought him farther and farther into her tight, wet pussy.

Baby thought there was no way Tammy was going to be able to take all of his dick, but Baby loved that she was trying. Baby stood there leaning against the dresser sipping on the remaining beverage in her glass as Treacherous's horse dick worked its way deeper inside of Tammy.

"Oh fuck!" Tammy cried out. "Oh, oh, oh, my God!"

Treacherous was Tammy's personal surf board. She began to grind on his wood. It eventually turned into a slow bounce. Baby watched with mixed feelings as she watched Tammy bounce up and down on Treacherous's dick. She didn't know if she wanted to continue to watch, yank Tammy up off of her man and kick her ass out, or join them. She sided with watching as Tammy's perfect breasts jiggled with each bounce she made on Treacherous's hardness.

Treacherous's full length was now engulfed in Tammy's pussy. She tried to conceal her screams of passion but she found herself actually panting. Treacherous didn't make love nor take his time with her. He straight-up fucked her. He wanted her to know that this was just meaningless sex. Tammy had never had that much dick inside of her in her life. Out of nowhere, Treacherous's strokes got faster.

"Aaaawww shit!" Treacherous bellowed. He grabbed Tammy by the waist and tossed her off of him. He then stood up and began jerking his shaft. Baby watched from the bed in awe as Tammy dropped to her knees and positioned herself in front of Treacherous's dick.

"Fuck!" Treacherous cursed as his juices shot out and exploded all over Tammy's face.

"Umm, yeah," Tammy moaned. She licked her lips to clear them of Treacherous's sexual residue.

Treacherous sidestepped her and made his way over toward the bed. Baby lay there playing with herself and began to get lost in the rhythm of her own fingers. She was so consumed with pleasuring herself that she didn't even notice Treacherous's sudden presence on the bed. When Baby opened her eyes, Treacherous was between her legs. He wasted no time diving in head first and exploring Baby's love cave. Baby tossed her head back and closed her eyes. Neither of them ever noticed Tammy gathering up her clothes and making her way to the bathroom. It wasn't until Treacherous had heard the room door open that he looked back to see the remainder of Tammy's backside disappearing out of the room as the door shut behind her.

"What's wrong?" Baby asked in a whimpering manner. The tongue lashing Treacherous was delivering had her gasping for air.

"Nothing," Treacherous replied with a sinister look in his eyes. Baby inhaled as his lips wrapped around her clit.

For another thirty minutes, Treacherous and Baby kissed, sucked, explored, and pleasured each other until they were both exhausted. Baby peered up at Treacherous.

"I don't ever want to fuck another woman again," she stated with conviction.

Treacherous looked down at her and smiled. "Okay."

"And, I don't ever want you fucking another one either!" she added.

He kissed her on top of the forehead. "Okay."

Chapter Nineteen

Sammy Black Jr. sat back and watched as a cloud of dust trailed behind the approaching vehicle. The unmarked car pulled alongside the black SUV with tinted windows in the open dirt field, facing the opposite direction. Neiko rolled down his window but kept the air conditioner blowing.

The back window of the SUV slid down. "Nice weather we're having." Sammy Black Jr. nodded.

"Too fucking hot, ya ask me," Neiko replied.

Sammy chuckled. "Yeah, it is," Sammy agreed. "So, what was it you couldn't tell me over the phone?" Sammy Black's tone came across as anxious. "What you got for me?"

Neiko answered his question by extending a piece of paper out of the driver's window. Sammy Black reached out and grabbed hold of the piece of paper. He unfolded the white sheet and peered at the writing on it. He stared at the numbers and words for a few more seconds then directed his attention to Neiko Bellini. "Is this what I think it is?" Sammy Black asked.

"I aim to please." Neiko Bellini beamed.

"This will never be forgotten." Sammy Black waved the white piece of paper in the air.

It had been over a week since he had heard from Neiko Bellini and was starting to get worried. The trail had seemed to become cold but Neiko Bellini had just turned the heat back on. Sammy Black Jr. flashed Neiko Bellini the Cheshire cat smile to show just how much the information he had handed him meant.

Neiko Bellini nodded and winked. He then made a saluting gesture at Sammy Black Jr. before peeling off in his unmarked car. Sammy Black Jr. rolled up his window to avoid the dirt residue from Neiko Bellini's unmarked car invading the back seat of the SUV.

"Drive!" he instructed. The driver did as he was told.

Sammy Black Jr. pulled out his cell phone. The call was answered on the first ring. "I got something for you. Take this address down." Sammy recited the address on the piece of paper then abruptly hung up. He ripped the white piece of paper up into as many little pieces as he could and cracked the SUV's window. He let the small pieces of paper blow out of his hand and fly into the wind. *Time is running out for you two.* He leaned back, propped his elbow up on the armrest, and peered out the SUV's window. *Yeah, time is running out.* He repeated his thought as the SUV floated through the open dirt field.

Chapter Twenty

What would be considered the best time of Treacherous's and Baby's lives was sadly coming to an end. Today was their last day in Miami and Baby had plans for the two of them. She had told Treacherous the previous night that she wanted to know what it felt like to just shop and have fun without caring about the cost. She knew it was just a matter of time before everything came to a screeching halt, and she knew they couldn't take it with them. Baby slipped on her new Chanel sunglasses she had just purchased as she trailed behind Treacherous. She nearly ran into the back of him when they exited the designer store.

"Bae, what's wrong?" a concerned Baby asked. She had noticed that Treacherous had cautiously looked in both directions each time they had exited a store, for the third time today.

Treacherous leaned toward Baby. "I think we're being followed. I been having this feeling all day. I feel like we're being watched."

"Are you serious?" His words caught Baby by surprise.

"Yeah, I'm serious," he confirmed. "Maybe we should get the fuck out of here tonight. I got a sixth sense for trouble."

Baby grabbed hold of his hand. "Bae, everything is fine. No one is following us. We're all the way in motherfuckin' Miami. Neither one of us knows anyone here. I thought we were going to leave all of our problems back in Virginia. It's just paranoia." Baby sighed.

Treacherous grimaced. "Everything just seems too perfect, you know?"

"That's because right now it is!" Baby exclaimed. This was their last night in Miami and she wanted to savor the moment. She was not ready to return to reality. She had been floating on cloud nine all weekend and didn't want it to end. "I feel it too, babe." She smiled. "For the first time in a long-ass time, shit feels right! We good," she bellowed. "We got money and we got each other and that's all that matters."

Treacherous listened with no interruption. Baby smiled again. "Listen, bae, I know that good things in your life always come to a quick and abrupt end and you had a fucked-up life, but I'm here, baby. I'm not going anywhere. Never. That feeling that you're feeling is a feeling of peace and contentment. Just embrace it, baby. Relax," Baby assured him.

Treacherous inhaled then exhaled. *Maybe she's right.* Things did seem too good to be true. The feeling was foreign to Treacherous. The more Baby talked the more he warmed up to just focusing on the moment, but he just couldn't shake the eerie feeling he had been having all day, since they had left the hotel. Something just didn't sit right with him. He knew they were far away from home, but it still didn't convince him that they weren't being watched. The entire time they shopped and enjoyed the day, Treacherous constantly was looking over his shoulder. He promised Baby that he would leave all of their problems in Virginia and enjoy the end of what was a weekend. Treacherous threw his arm around Baby's neck.

"You're right, bae." He smiled.

For the rest of the day they shopped, ate, went to the water park, rode rides, and played games all day. They were having so much fun that Treacherous erased the notion that someone was following them earlier. By the time they returned to their hotel room, they were both worn out. They dreaded the fact that they had to pack.

The fairytale life they had been living all weekend came to an abrupt halt. Treacherous shifted the bags he was carrying in his left hand over to his right and inserted the room key in the electronic lockbox. He held the door for Baby, who entered the room. What happened next happened so fast, neither Treacherous nor Baby had time to react.

Treacherous was the first one to regain consciousness. His vision was blurry and he had a headache that had Excedrin written all over it. He grimaced and grabbed hold of the area where he had been hit in the head with the metal barrel part of his assailant's gun. Had it not been for the shot that was fired as he was struck, he would have thought he had been hit with a pipe of some sort. The explosion next to his ear still had it ringing. He flinched as his hand made contact with the open wound in the back of his head. He could feel the dried-up blood and puss that oozed out of the gash and onto the back of his head.

He was still trying to decipher what had actually happened. He remembered holding the door open for Baby before he saw her go crashing to the floor. The next thing he remembered was the blow that sent him plunging on top of her. Treacherous tried to focus. His vision began to return. The first thing that came to mind was Baby. He did a quick scan of the room. He noticed that it had been ransacked, but she was nowhere to be found. His heart rate began to increase. He tried to stand but his legs failed him on the first attempt. Once he regained control of his balance and was able to stand, he rushed to the room door and snatched it open. Both the car and their bikes were gone.

"Fuck!" Treacherous cried out. He couldn't believe this was happening. "Fuck! Fuck! Fuck!" he chanted. When he turned back around, he noticed the bathroom door was closed. For the first time in a long time, he was nervous and afraid. He cautiously tiptoed over toward the bathroom door. He didn't know what to expect.

Please don't let her be dead in there, was all he could think about. Just the thought triggered something inside of him. Tears began to form and spill out of his eyes at the possibility. Treacherous wiped his face and grabbed hold of the bathroom door handle. He turned the knob but the door was locked.

"Baby?" he called out as he jiggled the door handle. There was no response.

Treacherous became engulfed with anger. All in one motion, he threw his weight into the door. When it flew open, Treacherous's eyes grew cold. A gagged and bound Baby was unconscious and bleeding from the forehead and mouth. Someone had tied her hands to the shower rod. Treacherous grabbed the shower rod with one hand and held Baby with the other. In one yank, he tore the shower rod from the wall. He scooped Baby up in his arms and carried her out of the bathroom.

"Baby?" he called out her name for a second time. "Wake up, babe," he added in a loving tone. Still, there was no response. Treacherous laid Baby on the bed then went back into the bathroom area. He returned with warm and cold cloths. He wiped the blood from her head and mouth then placed the cold one onto Baby's forehead. Just then, reality set in.

Treacherous hopped up and ran over to the room's closet. "Shit!" he cursed. His eyes zeroed in on the closet's floor where the duffle bag should've been. His heart dropped into his stomach. Aside from the few hundred dollars he had in his pocket, that was all of the money he and Baby had left. His eyes shifted from the floor to the top shelf of the closet. Miraculously, the duffle containing the casino chips was still on the top shelf.

How the fuck could this happen? he wondered. He knew it couldn't have been the police, because they'd be in handcuffs, and he knew it couldn't have been anybody in connection to the heist they had pulled back in Richmond because the casino chips would be gone and they would be dead. Treacherous realized he was not paranoid or bugging out earlier. He was now convinced that someone was in fact following them.

Treacherous pulled the duffle bag full of casino chips down. When he turned around, he saw Baby staring at him. He dropped the duffle and made his way back over to her.

"You okay?" Treacherous asked with concern in his tone.

"Yeah, I'll be fine." Baby's voice was a little horse.

"What the fuck happened?" Treacherous asked hoping Baby could shed some light on the situation. Baby's facial expression to his question told him she knew something.

"That bitch! That's what happened!" Baby blurted out.

"Who?" a puzzled Treacherous asked. He had no idea what Baby was talking about.

"Tammy!" If looks could kill, when Baby spit her name, whoever the intended victim would have been would be six feet deep from her facial expression.

The mention of her name caused the hairs on the back of Treacherous's neck to rise. He couldn't believe his ears. She was the furthest thing from his mind, despite the fact that they had indulged in a threesome yesterday. *There's no way she could've done this by herself*, thought

Treacherous. He also couldn't believe that one white girl had caught them slipping the way she had. He couldn't picture her delivering the blow that had knocked him temporarily unconscious.

"Are you serious?" It was more of a statement than a question. "How the fuck did she—"

"No!" Baby corrected him. "She wasn't alone. She had two big niggas with her," she added.

"That explains it." Treacherous gritted his teeth.

"Explains what?" Baby asked.

"They took everything. All of our clothes, the car, and the bikes."

"That bitch!" Baby cursed.

Treacherous shook his head. "It's my fault. It's my fuckin' fault," he repeated.

"What?" Baby shot him a crazy look. "What are you talking about?"

Treacherous continued to shake his head in disbelief. "I brought her here." All he could think about was how Tammy had gotten to their room.

"Aww, bae, if anything, it's my fault." Baby threw her arms around Treacherous's shoulders. "You brought her here." Baby's words lingered. "Out of love for me," she reminded him.

She now felt bad. She became stricken with shame. She placed her head on Treacherous's broad shoulder and closed her eyes. It had never dawned on her who the blame belonged to. But the reality was that had she not been having the feelings she had been and expressed them to Treacherous, there would have never been a Tammy. At that moment, Baby's resentment and hatred toward her mother resurfaced. Baby released her arms from around Treacherous and threw herself back onto the bed.

"You did this," Baby cried. "You did this to me, you sick bitch!" she cursed her mother. She was in a blind rage. "I hate you! I hate you! I fuckin' hate you!" she ranted.

She banged her fists on the bed and began kicking and screaming hysterically. "I fuckin'—" She was zoned out so much that she didn't hear Treacherous or realize he was trying to calm her.

"I said chill!" Treacherous repeated for the umpteenth time. He hadn't seen Baby so spaced out since they had escaped from the mental institution.

The strong grip wrapped around her arms and the sound of Treacherous's voice brought her back to the present. Her once out-of-control breathing began to return to normal. Treacherous reached out for her. She welcomed his massive arms. Treacherous could feel her body jerking as Baby's tears soiled his shirt and dampened his chest. "Don't worry," he said in a reassuring tone. "We're going to be okay." He kissed her on the top of her head. "The last thing I need is you falling apart on me." Treacherous squeezed her tightly. "Don't worry," he repeated.

Baby broke free of him. She wiped her tears. "I'm good. I just had a moment."

"Okay. That's my rider." That was music to Treacherous's ears.

Baby forced a smile. She had fully calmed from the tantrum she had moments ago thrown. "So, what are we gonna do?" Baby wanted to know.

"Right now our options are limited." Treacherous told her. He had already starting thinking of a plan B once reality had set in. Treacherous stood up and pulled out his wallet. "But I'm hoping our first option will be the only one," he added as he retrieved what he believed to be their best option. Treacherous pulled out the white business card. He dialed the number and waited. After a few rings, Treacherous recognized the voice immediately.

"It's me, Treach," Treacherous answered Ghetto Governor's question. He hadn't planned on using the information, let alone so soon, so he was a little uncomfortable about calling someone he barely knew, not knowing what to expect. The reaction to his name set Treacherous at ease. Treacherous got straight to the point. "I need your help," Treacherous boomed into the speaker of his cell phone abruptly. There was dead silence for a second. The next words spoken meant everything to Treacherous. Ghetto Governor's response to his request was the one Treacherous was hoping for.

Chapter Twenty-one

The trip back to Virginia was a quiet and awkward one. Treacherous and Baby rode in silence. They had only exchanged a few words once when they had stopped for gas. Baby still felt guilty about what had happened to them back in Miami, while Treacherous was preoccupied with contemplating their next move as he navigated their stolen SUV on the highway. Baby slept most of the ride back. Treacherous's mind was a million miles away as he floated up the highway. Occasionally, Baby would wake to check on him and to see where they were. Treacherous's mind was elsewhere. Each time she awoke, he had the same blank stare on his face.

The last place she remembered passing was exit 74 for Dunn, North Carolina, which was why she was surprised to see the Virginia state line sign. The SUV coasted on the interstate as the speedometer approached five miles over the normal 65mph speed limit. Treacherous had been putting some work in behind the wheel as he traveled in deep thought. An eerie feeling swept through Treacherous as he passed the overhead billboard displaying the state's red cardinal on a branch and reading VIRGINIA WELCOMES YOU. For the first time since they had left Miami, Treacherous reflected on the situation back at the South Beach hotel. The whole ordeal still left a bad taste in his mouth. He knew he had to shake it off. *What's done is done,* he told himself in order to cope with the loss. He focused more on the fact that Ghetto Governor was in a position to offer them a way to get back on their feet. Treacherous had no idea what the offer entailed, but he had already made his mind up that he was accepting it no matter what. He gripped the steering wheel tighter as he stared at the speed on the SUV's dashboard. He hadn't realized he had been going so fast.

Baby had gotten a funny feeling of her own. She dreaded being back in Virginia. Despite how their trip had ended, Baby would take Miami over Virginia any day. But even if she had wanted to stay she knew she couldn't. Now that they were broke they had to return to Virginia. On what terms, was the million dollar question she wondered. They were wanted in Virginia and although they had been lucky so far, she knew the risk they were taking. It seemed like every time she closed her eyes, images of what had led to her being a fugitive from justice invaded her head. She was all too glad to be free, but at what cost, was what weighed heavy and the most on her heart. Distant memories skipped through her mind. As images of her life flashed before her eyes, Baby couldn't help but appreciate her right-hand and crime partner. Either way, no matter what he wanted to do, Baby had made up her mind that she was riding out. Occasionally, she peered over at Treacherous. Her heart warmed with each glance at him. She smiled at scenes that played in her head of her and Treacherous. *I love this man.* She smiled within.

Treacherous could feel Baby staring at him. His eyes shifted from the road over to her and back to the road. "What's wrong?" he asked with concern in his tone.

"Nothing." Another smile appeared across Baby's face. She loved the way his voice always made her feel. It sent chills through her entire body and made her feel safe.

Treacherous glanced back over at her for a second time. He was just in time to catch the end of her smile. It made him grin. He reached over and grabbed hold of Baby's hand. "I love you." He took Baby's hand and raised it up to his mouth. He kissed the back of it and winked at Baby before directing his attention back on the highway.

"I love you more," Baby rebutted.

Treacherous chuckled. The tension and awkwardness that once filled the air was now replaced with love and laughter.

The playful exchange relaxed Baby. She closed her eyes and dozed back off. Treacherous looked over at her. A huge grin was plastered across Baby's face as she slipped back into a light sleep.

He couldn't help but smile as he switched lanes. He knew his Baby was back to normal.

Treacherous veered off onto the exit. Moments later, he was cruising down the back road of the quiet neighborhood they had recently moved into. Treacherous pulled into the driveway of their place and threw the SUV into park. He had told himself he was going to get rid of the stolen vehicle as soon as they got back into the area, but, out of nowhere, exhaustion overcame him.

Treacherous rotated his neck from side to side, extended his arms, and yawned. You could hear his muscles popping and his bones cracking. He had just released 800 and some-odd miles' worth of tension as he stretched. He began to brush the back of his head with his hand as he continued to rotate his neck.

Baby massaged the back part of her neck and right shoulder. It had stiffened from the way she had been positioned in the passenger seat during her nap sessions the whole ride home. She looked over at Treacherous. She could tell he was sleepy. He always rubbed the back of his head like that when he was tired. She smiled lovingly. She had first noticed it when they were in the mental institution, and she thought it to be funny in a cute way. Aside from that, he had just driven them the entire way back from Miami, so it was only right that he be tired. By now, Treacherous was leaned over on the steering wheel holding the bridge of his nose. Baby thought he had dozed off for a second.

"You want me to get rid of the truck, so you can go in and get some rest?" Baby suggested. She knew they'd have a full plate when the sun came up.

Treacherous shook his head. "Nah, we can dump it in the morning before we hook up with Ghetto Gov. We both need our rest. We both gotta be on our A game," he told her.

Baby nodded in agreement.

"I don't know what he got for us, but, whatever it is, I want us to be ready to handle it," Treacherous added.

"Okay, let's go in the house." She was the first to exit the vehicle. She dragged herself to the front door while Treacherous struggled to get out of the SUV. He snatched up the duffle bag containing the casino chips from the back seat. Between being tired and the weight of the duffle bag, Treacherous had to use what little strength he had to lug himself and the duffle to the front door. His trap muscles were on fire from toting the duffle and his eyes were so heavy he was having trouble keeping them open. Without realizing it, he had dozed off. Which was why he hadn't noticed Baby backpedaling until he ran into her. The look on her face woke him up.

"Get back in the truck." Her voice was a tone higher than a whisper. Treacherous didn't ask any questions. Her facial expression was enough to let him know that something wasn't right. Baby's wide eyes and tight lips as she spoke alarmed him. He looked left then right in rapid succession while backpedaling to the SUV. Seconds later, he was backing out of their driveway and zooming back in the direction from which they came.

"What was wrong?" Treacherous asked Baby. She still had the same look on her face as she did at the house.

"The front door was cracked," she announced. "Someone's been in the house."

Treacherous's facial expression now matched Baby's. "How?"

"I don't know." Baby shook her head. It never crossed her mind that they could possibly be coming back to VA with more drama at their doorstep so soon.

Treacherous pulled out his phone. He hooked a sharp right up the street intended for the highway. Luckily he made a right instead of a left. Had he chosen the opposite direction, he would have been likely spotted by the two Irish henchmen who had trashed their home earlier and were told to return to the house and wait.

Ghetto Governor answered on the first ring. Treacherous went straight in as to the nature of his calling so late.

"There's been a change of plans," he started out with. "We're coming to you now," Treacherous ended. He knew there was no time to waste at that point. He didn't even give Ghetto Governor a chance to respond. Instead, he hung up. Then he pressed down on the circle on his iPhone 6S and commanded Siri to pull up the directions to Ghetto Governor's house.

Chapter Twenty-two

"Who is it?" Sammy Black Jr. barked as he made his way down the spiral staircase of his condo. He grimaced at the muffled response from the opposite side of the door. Sammy slid the chain off the latch, then unlocked the bottom and top locks of his condo door. He snatched the door open in an irritated manner.

"What can I do for you gentlemen?" Sammy Black Jr. asked in a sarcastic tone.

Arthur Love and Andre Randle looked at each other and then back at Sammy Black Jr. "Mr. Black, I'm Detective Love from the Richmond PD and this is Chief Randle of the Norfolk PD," Arthur Love introduced them, embellishing Andre Randle's title. Both men flashed badges.

Sammy knew these were the cops Neiko Bellini had warned him about. He released a deep sigh and rolled his eyes. "Okay, what's this all about?" he asked.

"May we please come in?" Love asked. "We have a few questions to ask you regarding a homicide investigation in connection with the death of your father," he informed him.

Sammy Black Jr. let out a light chuckle. "Did you catch the pieces of shit who killed him?" Sammy Black Jr. asked already knowing the answer. His statement was more of a jab at Arthur Love. He could tell he caught it based on the knot on the side of his left cheek indicating clenched jaws. He knew Arthur Love's daughter was one of the ones responsible for his father's demise.

"No, not yet." Love kept his composure.

"Well then, we have nothing to talk about." Sammy Black Jr. started closing the door.

Andre Randle stuck his foot in the doorway to prevent the door from closing. "If we can just get a minute of your time . . ." he tried to reason with Sammy Black Jr.

Sammy looked down at his foot then back up at him. A sinister grin appeared across his face. "What I will do is give you one minute to move your foot," he rebutted sternly but calmly.

"So, you're not at all interested in wanting to find out what we've found out?" Randle stared at Sammy Black.

Sammy met his stare. "No," he abruptly shot back. "Let me know when you've apprehended them. Now, your minute is almost up," he reminded him about his foot blocking his door.

"Thirty-three, thirty-two," Randle began to count down out loud. He didn't take too kindly to threats. Especially from thugs posing as businessmen.

Sammy's eyes grew cold, but he never broke his stare. *The nerve of this nigger.* He was already calculating his next move in case he didn't move his foot and felt froggy and wanted to leap. He made one last attempt to get the officer to move his foot from his doorway.

"If you don't have any information about my father's killers or have a warrant for my arrest, then I strongly suggest you both get the hell off of my property! Now!" Sammy Black spat in a disrespectful tone.

That was all Randle could take. He already envisioned grabbing Sammy Black Jr. by the throat and shaking him like a rag doll until he stopped breathing. The one thing he did not tolerate was disrespect and Sammy Black had crossed that line.

Arthur Love could feel the tension between him and his partner. He could see in Andre Randle's face that he was on the verge of doing something he knew he'd later regret.

"Come on, partner." Love tapped Randle on the shoulder. He motioned to him with his head for them to leave. The last thing he wanted was for him and Sammy Black Jr. to get into a physical altercation. Neither of them seemed to be backing down from the other.

Randle stared at Sammy Black Jr. for a few more seconds. He then let out a light chuckle before making an about face. Love let out a sigh of relief. He knew he'd have a hard time explaining if something jumped off between the two. He made his way down Sammy Black Jr.'s ramp. Andre Randle followed.

Sammy Black made an attempt to close his condo door for a second time.

"Oh, one more thing?" Randle spun around. "You wouldn't happen to know anything about a young Irish kid getting killed at a motel would you?"

"Go fuck yourself!" he replied then slammed the door behind them.

"Didn't think so." Randle chuckled again. Arthur Love shook his head.

Sammy Black Jr. watched from the side window as the two cops made their way back to their vehicle. Once the car pulled off, he pulled out his phone.

"What in the hell got into you back there? You could've jeopardized the case," Arthur Love pointed out, getting in the driver's seat. He couldn't wait to get his partner alone to tear into him.

"Fuck that scum bag!" Randle boomed. "My gut is telling me that that asshole was expecting us."

Arthur Love felt the same way as Randle, but they were in two different positions. Andre Randle was no longer a police officer. Arthur Love was. He knew he had a responsibility to uphold the law at all costs and couldn't

handle matters from a personal perspective. It was bad
enough he was not supposed to be taking Randle with
him on any investigations. But they had started this together and that's how he intended to finish it.

"Let it go," he told Randle. "He knows we're on to him.
Maybe he'll call off his dogs and let us do our job now."
Arthur Love was hopeful.

"Yeah, maybe," he dryly replied. "But I doubt it."

Arthur Love put the Impala in reverse and backed out
of Sammy Black Jr.'s driveway.

At the same time, the caller on the other end of Sammy
Black Jr.'s phone picked up. "Yeah, those two fucking
detectives you told me about just left my damn house!"
Sammy had become angry all over again from the brief
brush with the two detectives. "We need to talk, and not
over the phone, so I suggest you wake the hell up and
get over here!" he demanded before hanging up and tossing his phone up against the wall.

Chapter Twenty-three

Ghetto Governor stood in his doorway with an unlit cigar dangling from his mouth and a full-length robe and slippers on. He watched as Treacherous and Baby exited the SUV. He welcomed them with open arms.

"Sorry about this," Treacherous apologized for waking Ghetto Governor up in the middle of the night.

Ghetto Governor glanced down at his Movado watch. The big hand rested where the number six would have been while the little hand sat where the number four would have been. "Man, don't worry about it. I was gettin' up in another hour anyway." He patted Treacherous on the shoulder.

"Thank you." Baby waved and smiled appreciatively.

Ghetto Governor nodded and winked. Once inside, he directed his attention to Treacherous. "Yours?" he asked, referring to the SUV.

"Nah." Treacherous shook his head.

Ghetto Governor chuckled. "Give me the keys. I'll have somebody take care of it."

Treacherous tossed him the keys.

Ghetto Governor stuck his hand into the right pocket of his robe. He pulled out his cell phone and placed a call. "Yo, I need you to come home and take out this trash if you want your allowance this week," Ghetto Governor chimed into the speaker of his Android. He spoke over the phone in a code that the man on the other end of the call understood. Both Treacherous and Baby deciphered that Ghetto Governor was telling the caller to come and get rid of the SUV.

"And, I need you to drop off a package for me at the post office on your way to work," Ghetto Governor added.

Treacherous and Baby looked at each other with puzzled looks. They couldn't figure out the second part of the code.

Ghetto Governor concluded the call. "We can talk in the morning," he said to them. "You guys need your rest, so you can fill me in on everything then," Ghetto Governor suggested. "And in case you were tryin'a figure it out," he said, changing subjects, "this is a nosey neighborhood. A Crime Stoppers, Say No to Drugs type of community, so it wouldn't be in none of our best interests to risk y'all staying here. So, I told my partner I needed him to take y'all, being the package, to my other spot on his way back home, which is where he works from, because it's going his way." Ghetto Governor shot them both winks. "He'll be here shortly. Here's the key." Ghetto Governor handed the key chain with the single key on it to Treacherous.

"I see y'all in the a.m." Ghetto Governor waved as he made his way up the steps leading to his bedroom.

Chapter Twenty-four

Baby was in a deep sleep, but the smell of food awakened her from the relaxing dream she was having. It was nothing extraordinary but it was enough for her not to want to wake from the dream. She had just been dreaming about her and Treacherous being on a remote paradise island with more money than she knew what to do with. She and Treacherous were no longer on the run and they were finally free to simply be.

Baby rolled over and smiled before opening her eyes to be faced with reality. She opened her eyes to the sun peeking through the blinds. She looked over at the clock that sat on the nightstand and it read 9:45 a.m. She couldn't believe she had slept in so late, let alone at all. Although she and Treacherous were appreciative that Ghetto Governor had housed them in his spare home, it was not Baby's home. She still hadn't gotten over seeing how their place had been trashed. She had put a lot of love into the home and was a little shaken up and hurt behind the invasion. Baby shook off the thought. The smell oozing in the bedroom, coming from the next room, prompted Baby to get up. She dragged herself to the bathroom.

"Hey, sleepyhead." Treacherous raised his head up from the plate in front of him and smiled.

Baby walked into the small kitchenette and saw that there was a plate with eggs, home fries, and turkey bacon with a glass of orange juice sitting beside it. She smiled with her eyes. Not only had he made breakfast for her but her eggs were cooked perfectly with the cheese melting nicely on top, compared to his plate where he obviously had scrambled his cheese into the eggs. A smile now appeared across her face and widened. To the average person it may have been nothing, but to Baby it was everything. He had taken the extra effort to make her plate completely to her liking. It had been a long time since someone had done something thoughtful and simple for her. She hadn't felt that way in a while, not since before she had been committed to the mental institution.

It was times like this that made Baby thankful for the bond Treacherous and she shared. She had something that was her very own and that was the unbreakable bond that she shared with her lover.

She pulled out the kitchen table chair and wasted no time digging into the breakfast.

"How's the food?"

"I haven't said a word since sitting down; that should be an indication," Baby slyly remarked.

Treacherous shook his head at her smart remark.

"But to answer your question, it's great," she replied in between bites of food.

"You know we have a big day ahead of us."

"Uh huh," she answered with a mouthful of food. *How could I forget?* She knew the reality of the lives that they lived. Since breaking out of the mental institution, there hadn't been a dull moment, to say the least. It was a trying time for them. Baby was aware that every day was a risk and one wrong move or slip-up may cause it to be their last day of freedom.

Baby knew that after eating she had to shower and get dressed. She knew they needed to get some money and that meant the only way they knew how. The Miami trip had still left a bad taste in their mouths. Baby still couldn't believe they had been caught slipping. She was still trying to convince herself it wasn't her fault. Treacherous continued to assure her that it wasn't, but she knew if he hadn't been trying to cater to her by bringing Tammy to their room, they wouldn't be in the financial predicament they were in.

Normally Baby had a no-fear attitude but today she had butterflies, a feeling that she would never reveal, but it was still something that plagued her. The job seemed to be very simple, based on how Ghetto Governor ran it down. "In and out type of job with no surprises," was the way Ghetto Governor had described the score. But Baby was fully aware that nothing was ever simple as it seemed. She hoped it was in fact that simple though.

Baby drank the last bit of orange juice in her glass then stood up. She made her way over to Treacherous and grabbed his plate. She placed the dishes in the sink then made her way back over to Treacherous.

"Thanks for breakfast." Baby kissed him on the top of his head. "I'ma go get ready," Baby then announced. She spun and turned. The impact of Treacherous's hand smacking her on her voluptuous bottom caused Baby to jump. Baby turned back around, rolled her eyes, and smiled.

"Hurry up." Treacherous returned her smile. "So we can get this money!" he added.

"I know," Baby agreed. "And we will." Then she disappeared into the bedroom.

Chapter Twenty-five

The sophisticated Caucasian woman strutted out of the establishment with a "satisfied customer" look plastered across her face. Treacherous and Baby watched from afar. After watching the flow of traffic in and out of the store they knew she was the last one in the store.

"Here we go." Treacherous looked back at Baby. She nodded and flipped her visor down. Treacherous put the bike into first gear. Within seconds he was pulling alongside the curb of the store. The layout of the store was simple, just the way Ghetto Governor had described. The doors were regular, not bolt lock doors, so they couldn't lock from the inside.

Baby was the first to walk in, dressed in an all-navy two piece and six-inch heels. Treacherous trailed a short distance behind. As soon as they walked in, their eyes lit up. When Ghetto Governor first told them about the small store and what he believed would be the take on the job, Treacherous and Baby were a little skeptical, but they were desperate and needed the cash. Now seeing the array of pieces with their own eyes, it seemed too good to be true.

Baby pulled her mask down. Treacherous took one last look out the door and saw the sophisticated Caucasian woman pull out of the parking lot from around the side. He drew his mask over his face as well. The first case to their left contained women's necklaces, earrings, and beads. The second display case was where the money was located. It contained men's and women's Rolexes from Yacht-Master to Presidential. The third display case had three trays of engagement rings. Treacherous and Baby couldn't believe the store only had one camera centered in the middle that didn't rotate. It just like Ghetto Governor had said. They couldn't believe he was also right when it came to the protection of the store. There was no security guard in sight.

Treacherous was armed with a gym bag and a mallet while Baby possessed two matching .40-calibers.

Baby sprang into immediate action. "Y'all know what the fuck it is! Put ya fucking hands in the air, bring y'all old asses over here, and lie on the floor with ya hands behind ya heads! If you wanna die do something stupid!" Baby yelled brandishing her ratchet.

The glass shattered, as Treacherous wasted no time smashing and grabbing the goods. He broke both display cases with his mallet and then started emptying them out while Baby held the store workers at gunpoint. Ghetto Governor had called what Treacherous was doing "smash and grab," something he had learned about back in New Jersey a long time ago. Treacherous and Baby had never heard of it. You couldn't tell by the way Treacherous and Baby worked the store that they were rookies at smashing and grabbing though.

Treacherous was snatching up watches and rings at a rapid pace. His motivation was not only to make it out of the store with everything but to get out as soon as possible. The jewelry store consisted of two elderly women and a middle-aged man. The two elderly women nervously walked to the center of the store with their hands up, while the man came from behind the counter and followed. Both women were in their early eighties, with gray hair done up Barbara Bush style and wrinkly faces. They looked like they had one foot in and one foot out of the grave. Treacherous was surprised they didn't have heart attacks right then and there. The man, on the other hand, looked younger than his fifty-two years of existence, thanks to eating healthy and working out. No matter how much he worked out, he knew better than to play the hero and try something stupid.

"Please don't kill us! Please!" one of the elderly women pleaded as she passed Baby.

Baby shoved her in the back. "Do as you're told and you won't have no problem."

Just then, Baby's and the middle-aged man's eyes met as he came within reaching distance of his gun. Baby butted him in the face with her gun, immediately drawing blood from his forehead, and pushed him onto the floor before he had time to draw his weapon. She wanted him to know she meant business.

"Oh you tough, muthafucka?" she exclaimed. The blow sent him crashing to the floor. "I'ma ask you one time. If you lie, you die. You understand me?" Baby explained placing her right foot in the center of the man's back. "Now, get up! You," she continued, pointing the gun at the two elderly women. "Where the cash at?"

"In the back in the safe," one elderly woman blurted out. She wanted nothing more than for Treacherous and Baby to take what they came for and leave as quickly as possible. She didn't know how much her heart could take with all that was happening at that moment.

"Show me!" Baby ordered, waving her gun at the middle-aged man.

Treacherous peered at his watch and saw that they had been in the store for just under a minute. He watched as the man escorted Baby toward the back at gunpoint. Baby was deviating from the plan he knew. They agreed to get in and get out with all that they could in seven minutes or less, still leaving room to beat the police's response time of ten minutes. It was the same plan they had discussed and rehearsed over and over. He had already snatched up all of the watches Ghetto Governor had told him to focus on so there was no need for Baby to want to go in the back. He took another glance down at his watch. A minute and a half more had gone by.

"Come on," Treacherous said under his breath as his eyes stayed locked on the back room door.

Meanwhile, Baby held the middle-aged man at gunpoint. "Hurry the fuck up!" she barked. She figured it would be easy for her to grab the money from the back as an extra incentive for themselves and snatch up whatever else was of some value. The middle-aged man wasted no time making a beeline to the wall safe they used to store cash and important documents. He was so nervous his hands were shaking. He struggled with the combination and was unable to open the lock in that condition.

Time was ticking. "What's the fucking combination, nigga?" Baby barked making him flinch.

The middle-aged man recited the combination. She shoved him to the side. In three motions, Baby opened the safe. She butted the middle-aged man with the back of her pistol, knocking him out. The safe contained cash and a few trays of expensive-looking assorted diamond rings. Baby grabbed the garbage bag out of the trashcan by the desk. She emptied the contents on the floor, and began putting the money in the bag. Just when she finished she heard Treacherous shouting from out front.

"Hurry up in there; we over our time by ten seconds. Let's go! Let's go!" Baby heard him bellow.

Baby stepped over the middle-aged man and made her way back to the front. When she came back she quickly emptied the display case with more rings.

"We good?" Treacherous asked.

"Yeah."

Treacherous nodded. He made his way over to the entrance and stuck his head outside the door to make sure there were no cops patrolling, or walking by on surveillance. He gave Baby the signal indicating the coast was clear.

"Stay down and don't get up," Baby boomed at the two elderly women. "Your colleague is in the back. You can go check on him after you count from a hundred to one, backward," she added.

Treacherous was already out the door. Baby rapidly made her way out of the jewelry store. Treacherous was already jerking the throttle on the bike and was in first gear by the time Baby hopped on the back. Moments later they were cautiously cruising on Interstate 64 all the way back to the crib Ghetto Governor had set them up in until they pulled the job off.

Although she showed him time and time again, Baby never ceased to amaze Treacherous. She continued to show him that she was a ride or die chick for real. He couldn't help but smile as he put distance between them and the jewelry store. *I found my Bonnie,* Treacherous thought as he exited the interstate. Seeing her in action back at the jewelry store turned him on. Treacherous couldn't wait to get Baby back to the crib. As he cruised down Waterside Drive, Treacherous couldn't help feeling like he had just pulled off a caper that could have easily been a scene straight out of his mother's memoirs. It was a perfectly executed plan.

Chapter Twenty-six

Treacherous and Baby walked into Ghetto Governor's game store storefront. They each carried small knapsacks over their shoulders. Ghetto Governor was engrossed in heavy debate with a group of teenagers about sports.

"Man, don't no Kobe got nothing on LeBron," complained a chubby brown-skinned kid with only half of his afro braided.

"Who told you that, young'un?" Ghetto Governor snapped back. "L.J. the truth!" he continued.

"Who got more rings?" a tall, lanky kid challenged.

Ghetto Govenor stared up at the ceiling and rolled his eyes. "Y'all don't know basketball. Y'all just know Jordan sneakers," he finally said, causing a rupture of laughter among the youth.

He spotted Treacherous and began walking toward him. Treacherous hadn't really noticed how big of a dude Ghetto Governor was until right then and there. He stood at the towering height of six foot three inches, and had to weigh at least 300 pounds, thought Treacherous. He had a huge, round belly that protruded far from his body. He had no way of knowing Ghetto Governor loved his stomach. If anybody ever commented about it, he would proudly rub his gut and simply say, "Good living." It was obvious that he was mixed with something, but nobody was exactly sure what he was mixed with. He would never reveal his racial heritage. He liked for people to wonder about him.

"What's up, bro?" he greeted him, wrapping his hand around Treacherous's and shaking it. "Hey, lady." He waved at Baby with his free hand.

Baby nodded.

The group of boys eyed and lusted over Baby's banging body as the three of them exchanged greetings.

"So, how'd everything go?"

"Just like you said," Treacherous replied.

Ghetto Governor's eyes lit up as he turned to the group of young boys. "All right, shop closed. Time to go."

"Ahh, man! We just got in here. It ain't even that dark out yet," they all protested.

"Get the hell out, you li'l knuckleheads," Ghetto Governor playfully growled, using his pointer finger to direct them out of the door.

"You fat bitch," one of them yelled, right before Ghetto Governor slammed the door in their faces.

"Ya mother," he called back, locking the door and hanging the CLOSED sign up. "Step into my office, brother man," Ghetto Governor said, heading to the back.

This was Ghetto Governor's favorite part. When he first put them down on the score, he was hopeful they'd pull it off, but he wasn't 100 percent sure. He knew there was millions' worth of insured jewelry in the downtown jewelry store and he wondered how much they were actually able to grab. Aside from the money he looked to make, Ghetto Governor couldn't wait to get a look and first dibs on a piece or two for himself. He had a watch fetish and was eager to see what Treacherous and Baby had come up with.

They entered Ghetto Governor's office. Ghetto Governor plopped his big body in an old chair. The chair whined and creaked underneath all of his weight. "Let's see what you got."

Treacherous plopped the knapsack he had in his possession on the desk. He unzipped the knapsack and started dumping the jewelry on Ghetto Governor's desk. Ghetto Governor's eyes grew as each piece spilled out of the knapsack and onto the desk. He expertly studied each piece with a critical eye, hefting them in his palm, trying to determine if a piece was hollow. He knew quality merchandise when he saw it.

Within minutes, Baby's knapsack had been emptied and examined. Ghetto Governor had all of the jewelry in front of him that Treacherous and Baby had gotten from the smash and grab. He caught a hard on as he computed what he could get for all of the merchandise. He hadn't come up on a lick so sweet since Treacherous's parents, he realized. *The apple don't fall too far from the tree.* It took everything in Ghetto Governor's power to keep his composure.

"This shit here," Ghetto Governor said, staring down at the other pile, "this is some grade A, quality shit."

Treacherous could see Ghetto Governor's excitement, but he wasn't interested in talking jewelry with him. He just wanted what he and Baby were owed so they could get out of dodge. The $7,500 in the safe, which they felt they had earned, was not enough money to float them. It wasn't even enough to furnish them with a new place. Outside of the casino chips they couldn't do anything with, they were basically back to square one.

"What it's worth?"

Ghetto Governor leaned back in his seat, putting his hands behind his head. He thought about it for a second. "It's worth a pretty penny," Ghetto Governor admitted. "But we ain't gonna get nothing near what it actually worth," he clarified.

"Okay, so how much?" Baby wanted to know. She too wanted to find out how much they could get and how long it would take to get their money.

"This over three hundred grand in jewelry!" Ghetto Governor exclaimed. "I can dump this quick and easy for one-fifty."

"How long?" Treacherous asked.

"Gimme about four or five days," he replied. He knew it would be no problem at all fencing the merchandise. What he didn't know was that time was of the essence for Treacherous and Baby.

Treacherous and Baby looked at each other. Ghetto Governor sensed something was wrong. "Is there a problem?" he asked.

"How much do you have?" Baby asked.

Ghetto Governor stared at her oddly. "You mean like, now?" he asked.

"Yeah, how much could you give us now?" Treacherous backed Baby up.

"Man, times is hard on the boulevard," Ghetto Governor sang.

Baby shook her head and sighed. She couldn't believe this was happening.

"Look, Gov. I know you have to be a good dude for my parents to have trusted you. So, I'm going to trust that you'll play as fair as you can now. We don't have four or five days." Treacherous waited for his words to sink in before he continued. Ghetto Governor's facial expression confirmed that he was now following. "Whatever you have access to that you believe is fair is fine by me, but whatever it is we need it now," Treacherous ended.

Ghetto Governor gave Treacherous's proposition some thought. He knew if he bought them out he could make more off the pieces by just sitting on them and pushing it in the streets. The white gold engagement ring alone was worth a grip, not including the diamond cuff links and solid gold Cartier watch, he thought. Ghetto Governor knew he could resell one or two pieces of jewelry and make his investment back. His brain calculated the profit he would make off this deal. Ghetto Governor's heart did some somersaults.

"I'll be right back," Ghetto Governor announced before exiting to another back room.

Ten minutes later he returned with a brown suede Polo book bag. "You got ya'self a deal, my man." He handed Treacherous the book bag containing $60,000. "That's my life savings," Ghetto Governor confessed.

"Not for long," Baby chimed in.

Ghetto Governor laughed. "You're right about that, sis."

Treacherous extended his hand. "Nice doing business with you."

"Same here, nephew." Ghetto Governor shook Treacherous's hand. Baby offered the same nod she had when she had first entered Ghetto Governor's establishment. She already started making her way to the front entrance. Ghetto Governor watched as she exited his store.

"Treach, hold up!" Ghetto Governor called out, just before Treacherous reached the exit.

"What's up?" Treacherous spun around.

"If y'all could use some more extra money, I got something else for you, if you're up for the job," Ghetto Governor offered.

By now, Baby had reentered the store. "Is everything all right?" she asked. She hadn't heard what Ghetto Governor had just proposed to Treacherous.

"Yeah, everything's straight. Governor says he got something else for us, if we're interested." Treacherous bought Baby up to speed.

"So, what is it?" Baby directed her attention to Ghetto Governor. Before answering, Ghetto Governor walked over to the front of his business and locked the front door.

"So, this is the deal," Ghetto Governor started out saying as he began to break down what was on his mind.

***

The walls shook as the concrete floor vibrated from the bass of the track thirty-two-year-old Marlo Williams bobbed his head to. He adjusted one of the switches on the keyboard and closed his eyes. The bass on the track increased. "I just wanna be the one . . ." Marlo listened, as a pretty, short light-skinned girl with an angelic voice sang into a snowball-shaped microphone. He gestured with his hand for her to raise her voice. He knew the flow of the track like the back of his hand and wanted her to bring her tempo up. After all, he had actually written the lyrics to the song and created the beat for it that she sang to.

"I just wanna be the one you need." The girl's pitch amplified.

Four young goons nodded their heads to the heat coming out of the speakers. The singer's melodic voice filled the half—million dollar studio's room in Marlo Williams's Petersburg home's basement. They were all in a zone themselves. For the past two hours, they had been in their boss's studio after enjoying a good day in the streets indulging in one of their favorite pastimes. They had all popped a Molly before arriving at Marlo's place. Twenty-one-year-old Kyle Williams, Marlo's younger brother, sat in a swivel chair up against the wall in front of a food tray, mixing red cough syrup with Sprite soda in spring water bottles while three other young thugs rotated three blunts of Sour along with assorted flavors of Cîroc and Rémy Martin. Once the concoctions were done, Kyle Williams distributed the liquid drugs. They all sipped on Lean as the pretty, light-skinned girl's voice took their highs to another level. They were all so engrossed in the music and drugs that none of them noticed the presence of the sexy female behind them. Heads were nodding to the bass and melodic sound of the female's voice blaring through the speakers.

Kyle Williams was the first to notice the surprised guest. He had just opened his eyes after letting the exotic weed marinate. By the time he was able to react, the unexpected shot to his left shoulder spun him around and pinned him to the basement's wall. It prevented him from retrieving his .38 revolver from the top of the speaker he sat by. The sound of the shot echoed in the basement. Everybody spun around in the direction from which the shot came. They all froze in time. Their eyes widened at the sight of Baby brandishing her .40-caliber.

"Turn that shit down!" Baby barked.

The music abruptly stopped. By now, Baby had one set of teary eyes and five pair of murderous ones staring at her. The pretty, light-skinned girl had her hands up in the air.

"Who the fuck are you?" Marlo Williams chimed. "And why the fuck you shoot my little brother?"

Baby moved in closer. She answered him with a blow upside the head. "Shut the fuck up!" Baby boomed. She grabbed Marlo forcefully by his shirt sleeve and yanked it downward. "Everybody get the fuck on the ground!" she then demanded as she took a step back.

Marlo Williams complied with Baby's request out of sheer fear. He had been in the game long enough. In his opinion, he believed that a hostile female with a gun would kill you quicker than a calm man with one and the last thing he wanted to do was trigger Baby off and lose his life over what he believed to be money.

Marlo cursed himself. He would have given anything at that exact moment to be at home with his wife of four years. He now regretted delaying his *Scrabble* night with his wife. Instead, because he had chosen his crew over his family, he was begging silently with his Maker to let him make it out of the basement in one piece.

So many thoughts ran through his mind as he cursed himself for not securing his studio and honeycomb hideout. He knew it was a setup. *Who?* he wondered. There was no way one woman could have the heart to singlehandedly come up in his spot trying to rob him. His suspicion was confirmed when he heard an additional voice in the room.

"I wish you would!"

The sound of Treacherous's voice drew Baby's attention to the right. Treacherous had entered the basement from the back door just in time. Luckily, it was unlocked, just the way Ghetto Governor had said it would be, or else one of the young goons he now had his twin .45s pointed at would have gotten the drop on Baby. He disarmed the two young goons who shared a futon.

"You heard what she said! Everybody get the fuck on the ground!" Treacherous backed Baby up.

Marlo did not recognize the voice. He tried to raise his head to get a look at the new addition to the room but found himself with a pistol aimed against the back of his head.

"Where's the money?" Baby asked. She cocked her weapon to let him know she meant business.

Marlo was waiting for that question. He knew if he wanted himself and everybody else to make it out of this situation alive he had to give up all of the money or else this was where they would meet their demise. The money was replaceable, but none of their lives were. Marlo Williams sighed.

"It's upstairs. In my safe," he whimpered.

"Where is the safe and what's the combination?" Baby asked.

"Behind the picture on the wall in my office. 3-3-74 is the combination."

The pain from the blow Baby had delivered when she first entered the basement was beginning to settle in. Marlo lay there bleeding from the head. He felt dizzy.

"You better not be lying," Baby threatened.

"I'm not," he managed to say. He had seen enough killers in his time to spot one when he saw one. He could see in Baby's eyes that she had killed before.

"Go ahead, babe, I got this," Treacherous assured Baby.

"You, get up!" Baby reached down and grabbed the light-skinned pretty girl by the arm. The girl was now on her feet.

"Noooo!" the pretty girl cried. "I'm not a part of none of this." She waved her hand around the room in a circular motion to put emphasis on her noninvolvement. "I just came to sing," she added.

"Well, right now you about to help me empty this safe, unless you'd rather I empty this clip in your pretty little face." Baby used the nozzle of her gun to brush the girl's highlighted weave out of her face.

The pretty girl cringed. Tears streamed down her face. "Please, no!" she continued.

"Bitch!" Baby pressed her .40-caliber up against the girl's temple.

"Okaaaaaaay!" she pleaded.

"Good girl." Baby pushed her toward the basement steps.

Treacherous rotated his pistols on Marlo, his brother, and his three young goons. Kyle Williams lay moaning on the cold basement floor. He was still trying to grasp the fact that he had just been shot by a chick.

"So, who sent you?" The question came out of nowhere.

Treacherous laughed. "We sent us. Now shut the fuck up before I send you somewhere," he added.

He glanced at his watch. He knew they had been inside the spot longer than they anticipated. His eyes kept shifting from the basement stairs to the five bodies lying on the floor. Moments later, he saw the red bottoms on the pretty, light-skinned girl's feet appear, followed by Baby's construction Timberland boots. They both were carrying designer book bags: Louis Vuitton and Gucci.

Baby flashed a grin only Treacherous caught. Then she shoved the pretty, light-skinned girl in the back. "Tie these niggas up with their belts and shoelaces," Baby ordered.

The pretty, light-skinned girl looked down at Marlo and the rest of them and then over at Treacherous.

"Bitch, don't look at him; pay attention to me!" Baby grabbed her by the face.

She pulled away. "Don't touch my fuckin' face!" she bellowed.

If she had more to say, she never got the chance to say it. Baby had aggressively grabbed her by the throat and shoved the barrel of her cocked gun into her mouth.

Fear was written all over her face. Her hazel eyes filled with almond-drop-sized tears. She regretted her words and actions, but knew it was too late to take them back.

"We not here for that," Treacherous reminded Baby.

Baby grimaced. She removed her pistol from the girl's mouth. The girl gave Treacherous an appreciative smile. Her smile was not welcome.

"Get your dumb ass down there and start tying these niggas up 'fore I change my mind," Treacherous spat.

The girl wasted no time dropping to the floor.

Moments later, all five men were tied up and Baby had just finished securing the pretty, light-skinned girl. But Baby couldn't resist. She stepped back to say something to the light-skinned girl: "Learn to speak when spoken to, not before," Baby hissed as she reached down and smacked the light-skinned girl across the face with her pistol, leaving the girl with a lesson. "That's for being disrespectful, you little bitch."

They all watched as Treacherous and Baby vanished out the basement's back door and into the night $175,000 richer.

Chapter Twenty-seven

Baby stepped out of the convenience store and onto the sidewalk. The sun beamed down and rested on the side of her face just as it start to set. The day began to wind down. She took in the final rays for the day from its beam of light right before the clouds moved in and swallowed them up. She stopped and lingered a few inches in front of where she had parked her bike alongside the curb. She pulled the bottle of Pepsi out of the store's black plastic bag, twisted the cap off, and took a swig. She had been craving an ice-cold Pepsi ever since Treacherous had fallen asleep on her. He didn't want her going out, especially without him, but she did anyway.

She knew that people were looking for them, but she felt caged in and just needed to get out. They had been hiding out forever, it seemed to her. She was tired of it. Which was why as soon as Treacherous closed his eyes she dressed and was out the door. She had expressed how she needed some space to clear her head but he didn't seem to get it. She found that to be odd. Riding always made them both feel better. She knew they were both under a lot of pressure and fighting their own demons within, just as she knew that aside from riding on open roads to collect their thoughts, they dealt with their stress and situations differently. They had been through and survived a great deal both separate and together. This was one of those times where she felt she'd be fine without him.

When the commercial had come across the television screen, Baby couldn't resist slipping out of bed, running to the store, and making it back before Treacherous noticed she was gone. It was a beautiful day, thought Baby. She wanted to enjoy some of it and her addiction to Pepsi was as good enough a reason as any to do just that. The soda felt good traveling down her esophagus. Baby nearly downed the entire sixteen ounces of fluid. Her body jerked repeatedly as she belched lightly from the carbonation. She removed the bottle from her mouth with a satisfied look on her face. Baby placed the cap back on the bottle. She closed her eyes and smiled as she let the Pepsi's aftertaste marinate. They immediately shot back open. An image invaded Baby's mind. The familiar scene came out of nowhere. Baby's mood suddenly changed.

She felt depleted and tense. The emotions of fear and guilt that she had buried resurfaced and rotated around inside of her. This was one of the demons she was fighting, which she just couldn't seem to shake or get over. Baby hated feeling this way. It had been a long time and she wished everything could simply be normal. She missed being normal; rather, she missed what her normal used to be at one time. She missed her life. Baby was in a daze. Her eyes were open, but the image of her aunt entered her thoughts again. It almost brought a tear to her eyes, but she fought it. She had loved her aunt. And missed her. In fact, she was the only one who she felt truly believed in her and loved her, unconditionally.

Baby closed her eyes for a second time. She shook her head and tried to shake off the miserable feelings that were creeping in. She leaned her head back, letting the sun rest on her neck.

The sound of a loud car broke Baby's trance. Her eyes shot open. She looked to see a black Hyundai Genesis with tinted windows pulling up behind her. The sight of the vehicle not only helped, but also forced Baby to shake off the unwanted feelings. The vehicle leisurely rolled into the empty parking space. The music that could be heard from the inside nearly drowned out the sound of the tires crushing the rock-covered field. Baby pretended not to be scrutinizing its every move, but she got on point. She gradually hung the plastic bag on the handle of the bike.

The black Genesis rolled into the space right next to Baby's bike. When the driver's side door swung open Baby stepped back. She was ready for whatever. Her hand slid to her side, where her Glock was concealed. She watched out of her peripheral view as a black heel and patent leather shoe appeared from under the driver's door. The five-inch heel was connected to a cocoa brown leg. Once the owner of the patent leather shoe finally appeared she stood behind the door of the Genesis.

Baby released the handle of her weapon and let her arm drop down to her side. Her facial expression changed at the sight of the woman. The vision of the girl had Baby stumped for a moment. She was beautiful, Baby thought. That familiar feeling made its way to the forefront of Baby's mind. She tried to shake it but couldn't. She was instantly attracted to the girl. Her attraction made her feel guilty. She had told Treacherous she was done and thought it was out of her system, but at that moment, Baby realized, it was not as easy as she thought to overcome her interest in the same sex.

She knew she should just hop on her bike and go, but something had her stuck. Instead, she stood there and studied the girl while she spoke with someone inside the car. Baby could hear the strong voice but could not see who the voice belonged to. Judging by the sound of the voice, Baby could tell it was another woman. She noticed that the girl had a weird look about her. She had eyes like a Filipino woman, but her lips and nose seemed to have come from a black woman from the backwoods of Alabama or North Carolina somewhere. She was shaped like one of them Dominican chicks you see at the strip club: thighs for days, enough ass to last you a lifetime, and breasts meant to be held gently.

"Damn," Baby said aloud to no one.

The two made eye contact after the cocoa brown woman finished her conversation. Baby never broke her stare. The patent leather shoes made their way past her, and Baby never took her eyes off her thighs. Baby thought about following the girl into the store. She stopped herself when she heard the passenger side door open.

"Is there a problem?" the occupant spoke.

At first Baby couldn't tell whether the person who was speaking to her was male or female. The fitted hat to the back, the wave scarf, and the big jeans all had her puzzled. It wasn't until she spotted the breasts showing through the bright yellow polo shirt that Baby was able to determine the gender.

"Who you talkin' to?" Baby asked.

"I'm talkin' to you."

"Yeah, okay." Baby smiled as she stepped back toward her bike.

"Yeah, okay, what? That's my fucking girl you eyein' down like that, bruh."

Baby debated whether to entertain or squash the potentially messy situation. She knew she could easily pull out her gun, brandish it, and the manly looking chick would duck back into her Hyundai. She knew it would be too risky and draw too much attention though. Besides that, how could she explain to Treacherous that she caught beef over some chick's chick? Especially when she had no business even looking at the stud's girlfriend in the first place.

"Look, no disrespect to you." Baby decided to bow out gracefully. "I had no idea you were even in the car." This was Baby's attempt to squash things. The chick wasn't having it. Her girl didn't make matters any better. She reappeared from the store, and smiled in Baby's direction, clueless to what was going on.

"What the fuck you smiling at that bitch for? Get your motherfuckin' ass in the fuckin' car. 'Fore I smack the shit out you."

Baby once serious demeanor changed to an amused one. She laughed at the stud. She thought it was funny watching this girl act like a tough dude.

She watched as the girl moved as fast as she could to get back in the car.

"What the fuck you laughin' at?" the stud barked.

That was all it took for Baby to return to herself. She was growing tired of the stud's aggressiveness toward her. She was not one to back down or bow out of anything. She had given the stud her one courtesy and she had refused it.

"I'm laughing at you, motherfucka!" Baby boomed. The stud never saw Baby pull her Glock from her side. "Now get ya fat ass in the car with ya bitch and take her sexy ass home before I split that fitted hat and take her home with me," Baby threatened. She couldn't resist. She knew that would add insult to injury and that's exactly what she wanted to convey. Hearing the stud talk to the girl like that struck a nerve in Baby. Baby couldn't stand anything that remotely resembled abuse. She could see embarrassment all over the girl's face and wanted to embarrass the stud in the same manner.

The look on the stud's face was priceless to Baby. She stood stone-faced and watched the stud get in the car. The Genesis began to back up. Baby mounted her bike as the Genesis pulled off. She laughed again as the sun hit the tinted window just in time to see the girl in the passenger seat wink at her and smile. The whole scene put things in their proper perspective for Baby. She may have had thoughts about another woman, but she only wanted one person: a man. That man was Treacherous. All she needed now was to feel Treacherous touch her and everything would be okay.

Baby threw on her helmet. She fed fuel to the engine of her bike. *Thank you, God,* Baby looked up and said to herself in reference to the close call. She was thankful that the altercation had been defused peacefully. Aside from that, Baby was glad no one had seen her with her gun out and called the police. At least that's what she believed . . .

Chapter Twenty-eight

A few days later . . .

"Richmond PD, Detective Bellini speaking."

"Uh, yes. Hello?"

Neiko Bellini noticed the nervousness in the caller's tone. He rolled his eyes into the back of his head and sighed. *Another freakin' prank caller.* "Hey, buddy, you know you can be charged for playing on the phone," Neiko Bellini informed the caller.

"Uh, yes, sir, I do." The caller's voice came across as leery and reluctant. "But this is not a fake call." He let his words linger. "This is about the girl you guys are looking for."

As soon as he heard it, there was no doubt in Neiko Bellini's mind what girl the caller was referring to. But he had to be sure. "Girl?" he asked in a more inviting manner than previously. He didn't want to scare the caller off. "What girl are you talking about, sir?"

The caller cleared his throat. "The one with the guy who's on the paper you guys passed out a couple weeks ago."

His heart began to pound up against his chest. "Are you sure?" he questioned the caller.

The caller went into his story about what he had witnessed. Neiko Bellini cut him off in midsentence. He grabbed hold of a piece of paper and pencil. "Where are you located, sir?" He jotted down all of the information provided by the caller then read it back to him.

"Okay, sir. Someone will be in touch to do a follow-up. Thank you for your community service." He hung up on the caller. His mind was racing like an Indy 500 winner. He knew this was the big break he needed. He was in the perfect position because he had information, information that came with a price. For years it had been the perfect arrangement. He had long ago stopped doing what he had been sworn in to do. Instead he made deals with the devil for monetary gain.

Something that was supposed to be a one-time thing had manifested into something bigger. It was a dangerous game but it was something he was willing to gamble on. Money was supposedly the root of all evil but this root had quickly grown into something much bigger. He believed this would be the piece of information that would set him and his family straight for life. He had come through in the past, but on nothing to this magnitude. This was the missing piece of a puzzle a few people had been working on putting together. He knew how valuable the piece of paper in front of him was. He pulled out his phone. The caller picked up on the first ring.

"I have something for you," he spoke into the receiver. "We can discuss the value later; write this down," he ended. After he had relayed the information over the phone, he balled up the piece of paper then shoved his phone back into his pocket. He lined up the piece of balled-up paper with the wastebasket. He cocked his wrist back in a basketball shooting position. Just as he was about to take his three-point shot, one of his colleagues popped his head up over his divider and broke his concentration. He spun around in his swivel chair to face the officer.

"The boss wants to see you," the officer announced.

He grimaced. "Are you effin' kidding me?"

The officer threw his hands up in a submissive manner. "Don't shoot the messenger," he joked before walking off.

"Psh!" He let out a gust of hot air. He could only imagine what his superior wanted with him. Whenever anyone was called into his office, it was never anything good. He glanced at his watch. It was just under ten minutes away from being his lunch break. *What the hell does he want?* he wondered as he gathered up his things. Whatever it was, he hoped it took less than ten minutes to find out.

Chapter Twenty-nine

Joshua Black lay back on the hotel suite's sofa, enjoying the oral sex being performed on him by the Russian prostitute he had ordered, while he puffed on a Cuban cigar. The woman stroked his hardness as her tongue rotated around it in a circular motion. She peered up at him with seductive eyes. A devilish grin appeared across her face as she sucked on the head of Joshua Black's dick like a lollipop. He looked down at the woman. Their eyes met. She toyed with him a little more, then took all of him into her mouth ferociously. He could feel her teeth scrape up against the side of his rod as her tongue pulsated on it. That turned Joshua Black on. He was into rough sex. He squirmed and moaned. He stared down at the blond wig bobbing up and down on him. She attacked his dick with conviction. He placed his cigar in the ashtray then grabbed hold of the side of the Russian woman's face and gripped it. He pushed the woman's head farther into his groin as he thrust his cock into her mouth. Joshua Black could feel her lips tightening around him as she took his mouth fucking.

The feeling drove him crazy. Joshua Black could feel that familiar feeling climbing. He arched his back and pressed the Russian woman's headed firmly onto his cock. He could feel her trying to break free of his hold to no avail. Joshua Black rammed the Russian woman's mouth vigorously until he had reached that point of no return. He continued with his thrusts as he exploded in her mouth. He could hear her gag occasionally. He released his hold of her head and lay back. To his surprise, the Russian stared up at him with a shit-eating grin plastered across her face. He watched as she soaked up any lingering sexual residue between his legs. Joshua Black's dick jumped. It felt as if he was getting erect again. In his mind, he was already anticipating screwing the Russian prostitute's brains out.

His thoughts were immediately drawn to the ringing phone in the case on his dangling belt. He reached down and grabbed hold of his phone. He pushed the Russian woman off to the side and answered the call. Before he could say hello, he was cut off. Joshua Black looked around until he found what he was looking for.

"Got it," he chimed into the phone after he wrote the information down given to him.

Chapter Thirty

Arthur Love sat in his office at his desk drinking a cup of coffee. He was still trying to digest what he had just moments ago reviewed in the file in front of him. He didn't know what to expect when he received the e-mail earlier from Andre Randle, with pertinent information that could affect the case with his daughter and Treacherous Freeman. He was thankful after Randle told him what lengths he had to go to in order to get what he had sent to him. He had also called in a favor and asked that Love be allowed to handle the situation in house rather than embarrassing his department by making a spectacle of the matter.

After reviewing the content of the file, he didn't know if he wanted to handle the situation on a personal level, a professional one, or both. He and Andre Randle both had their suspicions and now all was confirmed. Now it all made sense to him. More than anything he wanted to bring his daughter and Treacherous to justice, but the right way. *We took an oath,* he thought as he took a sip from his mug. He wasn't perfect, but there were things that a man wasn't supposed to do and it appeared lines had been crossed and trust was in question. Arthur Love sat and contemplated his next move. His attention was drawn to the sound of a ringing phone. "Detective Love speaking."

"Did you receive my file?"

"Yes, I got it," Love replied. He wondered how Randle had obtained the information. He admired and respected his detective skills and appreciated his friendship. He never ceased to amaze him. His police work made Love realize just how slow Richmond was in comparison to the seven cities of Virginia.

"I know that it isn't the news you wanted, but you needed to know," Randle retorted.

"Absolutely."

"The important thing is you have the information now. I'm headed over that way," he informed Arthur Love. "We gotta move on this now. Meet me at the address I gave you." He then ended with, "I'm with you, my friend."

Arthur Love placed the receiver back on the base and immediately got angry. He looked down at the file again. He shook his head in total disbelief. This was saddening to him. The new revelation had him speechless. But one thing was for sure: he wasn't going to pretend nothing was wrong or even attempt to downplay what was truly the problem. There was no doubt in his mind that the problem had to be dealt with. Arthur knew there had to be a major repercussion as a result.

Why? he questioned. He never understood why people chose the route they sometimes chose. Detective Love just wanted to know why. He'd been pretending all along that he was a team player, Arthur Love thought as he reflected on all that had transpired. That was half true, because he was a team player; he was just playing for the wrong team and could no longer be trusted, and as a result his integrity had been questioned. It was wrong on so many levels, thought Arthur Love. He tried to contain himself but his anger was getting the best of him. It felt as if the walls were closing in on him. Not sure if he was sweating because of anxiety or the hot joe in his mug, he was feeling delirious.

"You asked to see me, sir?" A head peeked in Arthur Love's office, breaking his train of thought.

Arthur Love just sat there staring at the face in his doorway. "Yeah, come on in," Arthur Love invited him.

"Actually, it's my lunch. Can it wait until after? I'm starving." There was a brief pause. "Or you could join me and we could head over to the deli and catch up and discuss whatever's on your mind. Wouldn't mind catching up on the case over a nice corned beef sandwich." Neiko Bellini laughed.

Arthur Love let out a light chuckle. "I'll pass. But this'll only take a few minutes," Arthur Love declined the offer. "Come in and please close the door behind you," he instructed Neiko Bellini as he took another swig of coffee. He peered up at Neiko over the top of the mug.

Neiko noticed the peculiar way Love was looking at him. For a split second an odd feeling swept through Neiko's body as he entered Arthur Love's office. *Why the hell does he want to talk to me with the door closed, and why the hell is he looking at me over that damn cup?* he wondered.

"Have a seat." Arthur Love gestured.

"I'd rather stand," Neiko opted. "I really am starving and this is almost my lunch break," he reminded him. He looked at his watch as he spoke.

Arthur Love shook his head. "I never suspected you for the type." He spoke with disgust.

"Huh? Type? Art, what are you talking about?" Neiko asked puzzled. A confused look appeared across his face.

Arthur scowled. *He really thinks he's smart and everybody else is dumb.* "You can drop the act. The jig is up!" Love spoke as he shook his head. He was still in disbelief.

"You are not making much sense to me. I just wanted to grab a bite and you are talking in riddles."

"It's amazing that you can stand here and look at me as if everything is fine."

"C'mon, man, what the fuck are you talking about?" Neiko became irate. He grew tiresome of Arthur Love beating around the bush. He had no clue what he was getting at.

Arthur Love's eyes shifted from Neiko to his desk. He opened up the mail folder and slid the copy of the file he had printed out in Neiko Bellini's direction. "I'm talking about this."

Neiko's eyes peered down at the open folder. The first line immediately caught his attention. A nervous feeling overcame him as he read the words: "Investigation on Officer Neiko Bellini." His armpits began to moisten. Without having to look up, he knew Arthur Love was staring at him, waiting on a response or reaction. He did his best to conceal his nervousness before he attempted to speak. "This is bullshit!" he spat. "Why would—"

That's as far as he got. Arthur Love could not contain himself. He charged at him like a bull. The impact knocked the wind out of Neiko and sent him crashing to the ground and his phone flying across the room. Love was now on top of him like white on rice. He straddled Neiko. He began delivering blows to his now covered face.

"You fucking snake," Love spat as he repeatedly landed punches to Neiko's forearms. "You know how fucking important this case is and you're running your damn mouth to Sammy Black!" he yelled as he punched him again.

"Whaaaat?" Neiko shrieked as he tried to duck the blows coming.

"Do not insult my fucking intelligence," Love warned as he began to attack him yet again, feeling unsatisfied. "I hope it was worth it, you piece of shit!"

"Fuck you, Love!" Neiko spat back as he regained his balance.

"No, fuck you!" Arthur replied as he managed to slip a punch through Neiko's forearms and connected. Blood gushed out of his now broken nose. He choked and gagged as the blood flowed through his nasal cavity and down his throat. He plunged to the floor. His head hit the floor, dazing him somewhat. A white piece of paper fell out of his once clenched fist.

The commotion in the office had drawn attention from others in the precinct. The office door flew open as two officers entered to break up the altercation that was taking place between Arthur Love and Neiko Bellini.

"Get him out of here and arrest this piece of shit," an out-of-breath Love screamed.

All the time and energy he and Randle had put into investing this case had almost gone down the drain because of Neiko Bellini. He didn't know the connection and didn't care. The only thing he cared about was that he had broken the code of honor and moral ethics. In addition, he was aiding suspected criminals in the pursuit and attempted murder of his daughter. All of those blows to Neiko's face and abdomen did nothing for the rage that was currently consuming him. He was glad his colleagues rushed in when they did or else he may have killed Neiko up in his office.

"What's the charge?" one of the officers asked, wide-eyed.

"Interfering with an investigation and tampering with evidence." Love regained control of his breathing. "One more thing," he continued, "conspiracy to commit murder!"

As soon as he mentioned the word "murder," Neiko Bellini's phone rang out. A nervous look appeared across his face. Arthur Love picked up on it. He walked over to where Neiko's phone lay and picked it up. He looked at the screen and then back at him. There was no doubt in his mind that the initials SB stood for Sammy Black. He also knew it wasn't what you knew but what you could prove. Arthur Love's blood boiled. The two men's eyes met. Neiko was the first to break the stare. His eyes shifted from Arthur Love's face to his feet before remaking eye contact with him. The average person would have missed it. But Love was not your average person. He looked down and noticed the balled-up piece of paper lying on the floor.

"Wait!" Neiko lashed out as Arthur Love kneeled down.

He paid him no mind. Instead, he opened the white piece of paper. It didn't take a genius to figure out that the call that had just come through on Neiko's phone and the balled-up piece of paper were connected.

"Son of a bitch!" Love cursed. "Get him the hell out of here," he commanded. Then he grabbed his jacket and keys and flew out of his office.

Chapter Thirty-one

The money machine rang off as it ran through and counted one of the stacks of hundred dollar bills piled up on the table. 100 was what the screen read once the stack of bills completed the process. Sammy Black Jr. stood and watched with folded arms. The machine in the secured back room took no time putting a dent in the ten piles of bills from the bootleg gambling hall Sammy controlled. Occasionally, his eyes shifted from the money machine to the surveillance camera monitors that patrolled the floors of the casino-style establishment.

Business was thriving as usual. The monitors rotated and switched locations with each blink of the screen. Table games from the common area as well as the high-limit section were all filled to capacity, Sammy noticed. That meant a lot of money was being exchanged throughout his operation. Any other time a huge grin would be on his face behind the turnout. This was how Sammy Black Jr. earned for the families. But no matter how much he took in, it still did not compensate for what was taken from his father. Sammy Black Jr. closed his eyes and grimaced. An image of his father being lowered in the ground invaded Sammy Black Jr.'s thoughts.

It's all my fault, Pop. He blamed himself and only he knew why. He played the tape back over and over in his head. *If only I would've stuck to the plan, things would have been different.* Sammy tried to reason with himself. He still hadn't come to terms with the fact that Sammy

Black Sr. only had the duffle bag of money and casino chips in his possession because he simply didn't feel like riding across town to secure them. Now, because of his laziness, Sammy Jr. was fatherless. He couldn't help but replay the last words his father had said to him that night before he had dropped off the money and casino chips and left. *"You can't be lackluster all your life, son,"* were the words that resonated in Sammy Black Jr.'s mind.

I promise I won't, Pop, he vowed.

The vibration of his phone on his hip canceled his trip down memory lane. He already had an idea as to the nature of the text when he saw the caller's name appear on his screen. He had given specific instructions not to contact him unless they had worthy information for him. Sammy opened the text message. The first thing he noticed was the photo sent to him. His eyes grew cold. Where there was once no reason to, there was one now. Sammy Black confirmed the photo and what to do next. He texted back rapidly as a huge grin appeared on his face out of nowhere.

Chapter Thirty-two

The larger of the two Irish henchmen scanned the area left to right as the black Suburban cruised down the downtown Portsmouth strip, while his partner played a game on his phone. He peered over at his colleague, whose fingers were moving a mile a minute, and shook his head. The information given to them by their boss led them to the unfamiliar area. For the past few days they had been patrolling the area to no avail.

"Hey look." The Irish henchman pointed to the left side of the street. The passenger looked up from his phone. Josh stopped what he was doing in the back seat also.

"What?" He was in the middle of sending a text message and wasn't paying attention. He hadn't even realized that they had come to a stop.

"Isn't that one of them?" the driver asked. He was pointing out the window to someone across the street. "Isn't it?" This time he tapped his partner on the shoulder.

The hit forced the passenger to stop, follow the direction of the driver's finger, and take notice of the same thing that he had. "I'm not sure," he said with hesitation.

"Well, be sure!" Joshua Black slapped the passenger upside the back of his head. He was now on full alert.

The passenger scrunched his neck from the sting of the blow. He flung around and shot Joshua a murderous look, but he knew better than to do anything other than just shoot looks. He knew exactly what Joshua Black was capable of. That's why they were driving him around and not the other way around.

"Is there a problem?" Joshua Black asked stone-faced.

The driver was trying to get his partner's attention to give him a look of reason. But the passenger knew. He cleared his throat. "No, not at all, Josh." His words came out a little choppy. "Let me see if I can see her better with this." He turned his camera phone in the direction that his partner had pointed and slid the slide to zoom in.

Joshua Black squinted to try to zero in on the female figure.

"I think it is." The passenger nodded his head. "Yeah, I think so. But I don't know. I'm not sure. Where's the picture? Let me see the picture." He stared at the picture. Both Joshua and the driver kept their eyes on the figure until the passenger confirmed. They watched the female figure seem to be going back and forth with another woman.

The passenger still was unsure. He decided to snap a picture to send to Sammy Black for confirmation. The men watched while waiting for a reply.

"Holy shit!" the driver chimed.

"Yeah, that's her," Joshua followed up with.

They watched as the female figure drew a gun on the driver of the Hyundai. A half a minute later a text came through his phone. "He said pick her up."

Joshua Black nodded. It took everything in him not to jump out and end her right then and there. Instead they continued to watch from a safe distance as the scene played out across the street.

"Look at this shit right here." The sight surprised the passenger.

Seconds later, the Hyundai had pulled off and so did who they were watching.

"Follow her," Joshua said.

Once the bike zoomed off they pulled out behind it. The driver made sure that he kept back by several car lengths.

"Don't lose her at the light."

"I'm not."

The light turned red just before the bike reached the white line. The two men watched Baby plant her feet on the ground.

"You want to get her now?" the driver asked Joshua Black. He waited for Joshua's response, looking at him through his rearview mirror.

"What you gonna do. Knock her off the bike?"

"Why not?"

"Not yet." Joshua shook his head. "Wait until she gets on the highway."

The driver frowned disappointedly. He didn't agree with Joshua's decision but he knew he had to abide by it. When the light turned green, he waited until Baby drove onto the ramp leading to the interstate. He continued to trail Baby from a safe distance. Minutes later, she veered off onto the next exit.

"Slow down," Joshua instructed him. He felt they were getting too close to Baby. The last thing he wanted was to tip her off to their presence. The driver did as he was instructed. Joshua saw the left blinker of Baby's motorcycle light up. "Okay, go for it," he announced abruptly. It was either now or never, he thought. The path she had turned down had given them the break and opportunity they needed.

The driver smiled devilishly. He scrutinized their surroundings. It was filled with mostly trees that stood in front of houses that sat back away from the main road. The lights were few and far between and it seemed like they were the only living beings out at that time of night. It seemed to be the perfect moment. Baby didn't seem to be paying much attention to them or anything else for that matter. They noticed that she was deliberately making the shape of the letter S with the bike.

The driver floored the SUV. "Look at this bitch; she don't even hear us coming." The driver was excited and ready to put Baby down. He gunned the engine. Within seconds the Suburban's speed had hit eighty.

"Come on, come on. Hurry up before she do."

"Fuck, look."

"Yeah, she seen you. Hit it."

The gas pedal of the SUV was now to the floor. This drew them closer to Baby.

Baby attempted to speed up again. The roar of the SUV's engine had come out of nowhere. She was in such a zone that she was oblivious to it until it was right up on her. By the time she could react, it was too late. They had already closed in on her.

She did, however, manage to retrieve her gun from her waist.

The front of the Suburban just barely tapped the back tire of the bike. That one tap caused Baby and the bike to tilt to one side. The jerk caused her weapon to fly out of her hand. Baby attempted to regain control of the bike to no avail. The back wheel was already into a full slant. The sound of it rolling across the tar was only heard by them and the trees. The metal began to scrape itself along the pavement, along with Baby's left leg and arm. The bike kept moving with no regard to her being pinned under its weight. The only thing that stopped it was the curb that it hit.

"Damn, she probably fucked up," the driver announced.

"You better hope she not dead," the passenger stated. "Or you will be," he continued with a chuckle.

"Go check on her," Joshua Black demanded. He found no humor in the matter.

The two men jumped out of the car and ran over to where Baby lay. They knew that they had to be quick. So far there had been no one on the road but they didn't know how long their luck would last.

The driver stood over Baby. He bent down and felt her neck. "She alive." The driver was relieved. He did not want to face the wrath of Sammy Black and lose his life over a mishap.

"You lucky," the passenger confirmed his thoughts.

"Whatever, let's get her up." The driver lifted the bike, while the passenger pulled Baby from under it. "Roll that shit over into the grass so no one can see it."

Baby was out cold. The left side of her body was completely scraped up and bloody.

"Come on, man, let's go. Go open the truck."

The driver ran back to open the truck. They tossed Baby in the back.

Joshua Black turned and peered back at the trunk of the SUV. He watched as the two Irish henchmen worked together to bind and gag Baby. "So, this is one of the niggers who robbed our family and killed my uncle," he stated more than asked. Still the two henchmen nodded as they secured Baby.

Once they were back in the SUV, the passenger grabbed his phone from the seat. "Sammy texted me back. Said he wants us to meet him at the pub."

Joshua Black nodded. He figured that's where his cousin would want to handle the matter. *How appropriate,* thought Joshua Black, knowing what the pub signified. "Yeah, let's go," Joshua Black instructed them.

He sat back and closed his eyes. As the SUV navigated back to the highway, Joshua Black prepared himself to get ready to do what he was known for and best at.

Chapter Thirty-three

Arthur Love stood listening as the young black cashier replayed the tape for him and Andre Randle. "And then what?" Arthur Love asked. He had yet to jot down anything pertinent on the notepad he held in his hand.

"Nothing really. After she purchased a couple sodas and some snacks, she left."

"Was she alone?"

"Yes."

"What was she driving?"

"She was on a motorcycle," the young cashier replied.

Arthur Love nodded. It sounded like Baby to him. "What made you call the police?"

"Well, I recognized her from the poster you guys had been passing around to local businesses." The young kid cleared his throat. "And the reward money really caught my eye."

Arthur Love raised his eyes from the notepad to the young cashier. Andre Randle let out a light chuckle. He respected the kid's honesty.

"We'll get to that if the information you provide pans out. So, what else happened?" Arthur Love continued.

The young cashier nodded. He was already leery about snitching for money, so he didn't want to press the issue. "She and another woman exchanged words in the parking lot."

"Did it result in an incident?" Arthur Love questioned.

"No, not nothing physical." The young black cashier paused. "But the girl did pull out a gun." He began chewing on his fingernails after he spoke.

"Which girl?" Randle jumped in for the first time.

The young cashier looked at him and then back at Love as if he was seeking approval to answer the question. Love flashed a grin and nodded. Randle fought back his laughter.

"The one you lookin' for," he replied. "That's what made me pay close attention to her. When she pulled the gun," he added.

Arthur Love wrote down a few notes for the first time. "What happened next?"

"I called and spoke with a Detective Bellini."

A look of disdain appeared across Arthur Love's face. The mention of Neiko Bellini caused the hairs on the back of his neck to rise. He maintained his composure still. "I mean before you contacted the police, what else happened?"

"Oh. That was pretty much it," the young cashier stated. "After she pulled that gun, the girl she was arguing with got back in her car and pulled off."

"You know which direction she went?" Randle asked.

"That way." The young cashier pointed to the left of him.

"Thanks." Love closed his notepad. "Anything else you can think of?" he then asked.

"Um . . ." The young cashier put his hand under his chin and looked to the ceiling as if it knew something he couldn't remember.

They were both growing annoyed with the cashier's slow-motion rendition of seeing Baby at the store. They did not want to pry but at the same time no one had time to stand there and pull teeth to get information that should have been flowing freely. They both hoped the trip would provide some valuable information that would lead them in the right direction of finally bringing Treacherous and Baby in.

Arthur Love pulled out his business card. As far as he was concerned, the interview was over. "If you can think of anything else, give me a call." He handed the young cashier the card then made an about face.

"Thanks. We will be in touch." Andre Randle nodded before doing the same.

"Kids these days." Arthur Love shook his head once outside the convenience store.

Andre Randle laughed and nodded in agreement. Arthur Love reached for the unmarked car door's handle. As soon as he got in the car and placed the key in the ignition, his cell phone rang.

"Hello, Detective Love here," he answered. He was met with a distorted sound and commotion on the other end of the receiver. He looked at the phone then placed it back up to his ear. This time, he heard voices.

"Hello?" Arthur Love boomed into the phone. His voice became more aggressive.

"What's wrong?" an alarmed Andre Randle asked.

Arthur Love threw up his hand to silence his partner. "Hello?" he repeated. "Hello! Is someone there?" Arthur Love questioned. His frustration was apparent.

Randle watched as Arthur Love became irate behind the call he'd received. The call ended and Arthur Love punched the steering wheel.

"What's the matter?" Randle was eager to know.

Arthur Love looked over at his friend. He sighed then took a deep breath. "I'll tell you in a minute," he promised. He scrolled through his phone until he reached the station's number.

"Yeah, this is Detective Love," he informed the dispatcher on duty. "I need to get a trace on a call."

Andre Randle sat on the passenger side shaking his head. It was killing him not to know what was going on.

"Okay, gimme a sec." Arthur Love pulled out his notepad and pen. He scribbled the address down given to him by the dispatcher. "Got it, thanks." He ended the call.

"So you wanna tell me what's going on?" Andre Randle wasted no time asking.

Arthur Love inhaled then exhaled. "I think that was my daughter," he confessed.

The look on Andre Randle's face was indescribable. "Who? What? How?" Andre Randle rambled. For some reason, he could not put his words together. He was just as surprised to hear who the caller was as Arthur Love was to be receiving the call.

"I think she's in trouble," he offered.

Andre Randle frowned. He knew there was only one person who could have Arthur Love's daughter. "You got an address?" he asked. He could see the pain written all over Arthur Love's face.

Arthur Love nodded.

"Well, let's go get her then." Andre Randle placed a reassuring hand on Arthur Love's shoulder.

"Yeah." Arthur Love nodded approvingly. "Let's go get her."

His words lingered in the air as he threw the unmarked car into drive and sped out of the parking lot.

Chapter Thirty-four

Treacherous jumped out of a deep sleep. He was sweating profusely and was breathing uncontrollably. The nightmare he was having had shaken him enough to break his catnap. He sat up. The bad dream seemed so real to him. The last thing he remembered was trying to keep his eyes on Baby, who was covered in blood, being put into an all-black SUV with tinted windows in handcuffs, while he fought to resist his own arrest. The blank blue screen from the forty-two-inch flat TV stared at him. Treacherous shook his head at the thought of the nightmare. He stretched and yawned. He felt restless and his body felt drained. He had just been watching the movie *Moves We Make* with Baby, after he had put down a huge plate of turkey spaghetti she had prepared. The food must have given him the itus he thought. He peered over to his side and noticed Baby wasn't lying next to him. He glanced over at the clock on the wall. Nearly two hours had gone by. He hadn't realized he had been asleep for such a long time. An eerie feeling swept through Treacherous's body. Even the room seemed to be colder than normal.

"Baby?" Treacherous called out.

There was no reply. He wondered how long she had been up and what she was doing that prevented her from answering him.

Treacherous stood and made his way into the living room. "Baby?" Treacherous called out for a second time.

He did a quick scan of the room. Baby was nowhere to be found. He did, however, notice Baby's helmet and riding jacket were not next to his. Seeing the items missing from where he last saw them refreshed Treacherous's memory. He remembered Baby had expressed earlier how she was thinking about stepping out. He knew she had a lot on her mind and felt she needed to take a ride, but he was against it. Although they had been out alone before, he always felt uneasy about her being out without him. Treacherous couldn't believe how far they had come. It seemed like just yesterday that he and Baby had met in the mental institution and had fallen in love. Every day felt like the first time he had just laid eyes on her when he woke in the morning. Now, here they were. Treacherous returned to the present. "Damn," he said out loud.

Another hour went by, Treacherous noticed. It only took him a few more minutes to realize that more than three hours had gone by since he had spoken with Baby last.

He looked out the window and saw that the sun that was out when he had first laid down was now replaced with nightfall. He looked at his watch. It confirmed the time that had passed. Treacherous's heart rate increased. He scanned the room for his cell. At first, he couldn't find it. He began to toss the place. He was about to throw a pillow across the room when it hit him. He had stuck it in his pants pocket earlier. He made a beeline for the closet, flung the door open, grabbed the jeans from the floor, and retrieved the cell phone from his left front pocket. Treacherous took a deep breath. *Come on, Baby, answer the phone,* he hoped to himself.

The first ring caused his heart to jump as it transitioned into the second and then third.

Fuck. Come on, Baby, pick up! He didn't want to think the worst but as the phone went into the fourth ring, he couldn't help but to.

"What the fuck. Pleaseeee." Treacherous cursed under his breath. Baby had never let her phone go past three rings whenever he called her so to hear it go past the usual alarmed him.

Treacherous hung up before the end of the fourth ring and dialed it back again. His adrenaline started pumping as he waited for the phone to ring. This time it went straight to voicemail. Treacherous stared at the phone and frowned. It was the first time he had ever gotten Baby's voicemail. *What the hell?* was the first thought to come to his mind. He could hear Baby's voicemail beep.

"Baby!" he shouted into the receiver. "Where you at? And why you not answering? Call me as soon as you get this!" Treacherous ended his message. He then took a deep breath to calm himself.

Once he had gained control over his breathing he paced back and forth in the room for about a good ten minutes. Then he called her number back again. Still, same thing. He opened the front door of the crib and stood in the doorway. He checked the parking lot for clues or foul play. He scanned the row of cars. He even walked to the edge of the driveway to look up the street. He came up empty-handed.

He grabbed the back of his head and shook it in disbelief. He clicked on Baby's number and tried her cell phone once again as he made his way back into the house. He was met with her voicemail again. When she didn't answer Treacherous threw the phone onto the bed out of frustration as he entered their bedroom. The phone landed on the bed, bounced one time, and fell onto the floor. Treacherous didn't even bother to retrieve it.

All kinds of thoughts started to run through his head. It wasn't like Baby to not answer her phone or to be gone for hours without checking in. *Something's not right,* he told himself. He couldn't imagine and would not allow himself to think about why Baby was not answering her phone and what it could mean.

The inside of Treacherous's stomach began to twist into knots. His heart rate was now beating in rapid succession. The headache that was building was starting to take control over his thoughts. A sharp pain pulsated down the middle of Treacherous's skull and found a resting place to throb repeatedly on the left side of his temple. *If it weren't for bad luck we wouldn't have any,* Treacherous concluded, in regard to all he and Baby had been going through. He didn't like the feeling he was getting. Without his knowledge, a few tears escaped from the side creases of Treacherous's eyes. He didn't know what he would do if something happened to her. The tears were fueled by anger and not sadness. Murder was the only thing that came to Treacherous's mind in the event someone had harmed Baby.

He sat down on the side of the bed to collect his thoughts. The sound of his cell phone ringing made him put them on pause. He snatched it up quickly. The words **My One and Only** appeared across the screen. Treacherous let out a sigh of relief. Treacherous tried to calm his nerves. He shook his head and laughed to himself for overreacting. He answered with a smile.

"You had me going crazy in here just now." Treacherous wasted no time speaking into the phone.

His smile instantly disappeared and his facial expression immediately changed from concern to anger with what he heard on the other end of the receiver. The voice caught him by surprise.

"Who the hell is this?" Treacherous boomed into the phone. Instead of receiving an answer he was told to shut up and listen. Before he could get another word out, the recognizable cries in the background caused him to think twice.

Treacherous's jaws tightened. "Fuck!" he cursed under his breath. "Motherfucka, if you—"

The cries grew louder as Treacherous made a failed attempt to threaten the person on the other end of the phone.

"Okay! Okay! What the fuck do you want?" Treacherous asked submissively.

He listened with clenched teeth as the caller ran down his demands.

Chapter Thirty-five

The two Irish henchmen abruptly ceased conversation at the sight of the maroon and gray Maybach that pulled up. The car seemed to appear out of nowhere.

The taller man of the two scurried over toward the back door of the luxury vehicle and opened it. "Mr. Black," he greeted him as Sammy stepped out of car with a metal case in hand.

Sammy nodded and buttoned the middle button of his suit jacket. He then made a beeline to the entrance of one of the many properties his family owned.

The factory building that had been abandoned for nearly a decade was a perfect setting for a crime to go unnoticed. It was a cold, dark, and gloomy place. All that could be heard was the sound of rats scurrying about the abandoned hallway. The building was completely unfurnished and had no electricity or heat. The walls were cement, as were the floor and the ceiling. Electrical wires and asbestos were hanging down from every ceiling beam. An abundance of blood had been shed in the building during his family's reign. That's all he could think about as he trailed the eerie hallway of the gutted building. This building was not only historical for Sammy Jr.'s family but was also sentimental to him. Since he was a young lad, he stood by his father's side and watched as he made examples out of violators in the room they called "the pub." Sammy Jr. had heard countless pleas, cries, and screams from some of the most allegedly ruthless and tough gangsters in the underworld. Some he was responsible for, but most were credited to his father.

A ball of anger arose inside of him as he thought about the fact that his father was no longer at the helm of their organization and not around to guide him any longer. What angered him the most was that he was just mere feet away from one of the people responsible for the demise of his father. Laughter met him at the doorless entryway.

"Oooh!" The two Irish goons chuckled in unison as blood shot out of Baby's mouth. They had been watching Joshua Black deliver massive blows to the head and body of Baby. Sammy Jr.'s younger cousin had been punishing Baby for the past hour as he waited for his big cousin and boss to arrive. The strong right hook to Baby's jaw was the third consecutive one he had landed. *She's a tough little nigger bitch,* he thought as Baby remained conscious despite the fact that he had hit her with some of his best boxing shots.

Baby raised her head and smiled. "That's all you got, you Irish prick?" she spat. "Wait until my boyfriend gets here," she antagonized Joshua Black.

Her words struck a nerve. Joshua Black was a full-blown racist and could not accept the fact that a black woman could withstand what no man ever could. He was certain the next blow he intended to hit Baby with would put her lights out.

"Your boyfriend, huh?" Joshua Black threw her words back at her. "Let's see if you can last that long." He shifted his weight back to his left side and pivoted. Just as he was about to throw his punch the familiar voice stopped him in his tracks.

"That's enough, Josh!" Sammy Jr. entered the open room. His tone was thunderous but his demeanor was calm. He knew his cousin was taking his personal emotions out on who he believed to be responsible for the death of his father, but Sammy needed answers. This was both personal and business for him. He knew he had to take care of the business side of things before he could think about handling things on a personal level.

He made his way over to where they had Baby tied to a beam. Once in front of her, he stared Baby up and down. Minus the bruises from the beating she had obviously been taking, Sammy thought Baby to be a pretty girl for a black girl. He could see that she was young. He wondered how she and her guy could have gotten the drop on his father. The thought of it caused his blood to boil. He wanted nothing more than to pull out his chrome Desert Eagle and blow a hole in Baby's face, but he knew that was not possible. *At least not at the moment,* he told himself. Sammy shook off the thought. He set the metal briefcase down on the floor then put his hands behind his back and moved in closer to Baby.

"Where is my money and casino chips?" he asked in a calm and mild tone.

Baby raised her head. She looked at Sammy Black Jr. "I don't know what you're talking about." Her words came out slurred. Blood poured out of her mouth and onto the concrete floor.

Sammy grunted. He revealed a sinister smile. "Oh, you don't know what I'm talking about?" he repeated Baby's words. Sammy looked over at his cousin and nodded. Out of nowhere, Joshua Black threw a crashing right hook to the side of Baby's head. The blow caused Baby's knees to buckle. Like before, a smile appeared across Baby's face. She continued to antagonize him.

Joshua Black had built up a hatred toward Baby. He hated how tough she thought she was. When they had first taken her out of the SUV and attempted to tie her up to the beam, Baby had managed to knee Joshua Black in the groin. She had also managed to almost disarm him, after he had bellied over from the knee assault and dropped his gun. Had it not been for one of the henchmen, he knew it could have gotten ugly for him and the two men. For that, Joshua butted Baby repeatedly in her face with his gun. He blacked out and delivered multiple kicks to her head and body once she had fallen to the floor. By now, his gun was flipped back upright in his hand.

"Whoa! We need her alive! What are you doing?" Sammy spun around just in time before Joshua fired his pistol. He was on the verge of killing her. Luckily his cousin had intervened, he thought. He knew it wasn't the right time, but he had let his emotions get the best of him for a moment. But right now, every chance he got he wanted to make Baby feel pain. He went to deliver a second blow but was waved off again by Sammy. This time he put his pointer finger up to his lips and shushed his cousin. A puzzled look appeared on Joshua Black's face. Sammy Black's eyes dimmed low. He tilted his head to the side.

"You hear that?" he asked his cousin, who had just heard what he had.

Joshua Black nodded.

"How the fuck did that happen?" Sammy Black then asked, "Nobody checked this fucking nigger?" he exclaimed. He moved back in closer to where Baby was tied up. "For all we know, she could have a fucking gun stuck up her ass!" he boomed as he stuck his hand in Baby's back right jeans pocket.

Joshua Black shrugged his shoulders. *She's a sly fuck,* Joshua Black thought, and wondered how the cell phone had slipped past him and the two henchmen.

The screen read My Life. "Aww, isn't this sweet," Sammy Black chimed in a mocking tone. "How do you guys say it?" Sammy Black smiled. "Your boo boo is calling," he slyly remarked.

He was sure it was Baby's boyfriend and crime partner. He sent the call to voicemail.

"Now, if you want to see Your Life again, you'll tell me where my money and chips are," Sammy proposed to Baby.

Baby laughed. She wondered when they would find her phone. She thought they had seen her pull it out and slip it back into her back pocket after she had dropped her gun. Just then her phone rang again. She raised her head for a second time.

"You might as well answer," she suggested. "He already knows I'm in trouble," she told Sammy Black.

Sammy smiled. He actually admired Baby's heart. Still, he believed no matter how tough she was, she was not ready for what he had in store for her. "No, you're more than in trouble," Sammy Black corrected her.

He sent Baby's phone to voicemail again. He then kneeled down and retrieved the metal briefcase. He tossed Baby's phone to his cousin then stepped over to an old rusted pushcart. He set the metal briefcase onto the rusted pushcart and opened it. Baby had pretended not to be looking, but she watched Sammy Black Jr.'s every move as much as she could with partially swollen and bloody eyes. She tried to see what was in the metal briefcase but from where she was tied up, she couldn't see the contents. But when Sammy Black turned to face her, her question was answered. The glint from the silver object brushed across Baby's face as Sammy Black twirled the sharp knife in his hand. Baby's attention was drawn from the knife to her ringing phone.

"Answer it," Sammy Black instructed his cousin.

On the fourth ring Joshua Black hit accept on baby's phone and pressed the speaker button.

Baby's heart nearly stopped beating at the sound of his voice. By now Sammy Black was standing next to her with the knife pressed up against her face with his finger up against his mouth again. He was now shushing Baby as they listened to her phone.

"Sorry, your little girlfriend can't come to the phone right now," Sammy Black replied on behalf of Baby.

He could hear Treacherous asking who he was. He was not in the mood for small talk.

"Just shut your mouth and listen," Sammy answered.

The phone sound distorted as Treacherous barked into the phone.

Sammy Black grimaced. His patience grew thin. He turned toward Baby. He roughly grabbed her by the face and pressed the sharp blade up against the side of her face.

"Aggggggggh!" Baby's screams echoed throughout the gutted building as Sammy Black slowly slid the blade down her cheek and made an L-shape incision. A thin trail of blood trickled down and followed the blade until it stopped a distance away from her right eye.

Treacherous's pleas could be heard through the speaker of Baby's cell phone.

Sammy Black released Baby's face and walked over toward where Joshua Black was standing, holding the phone. He leaned in closer to the cell phone. "What I want is my fucking money and casino chips," he calmly spoke into the phone. He gave Treacherous an address. "And you got two hours to make it across the water and get it to me in full or you're going to find your little pretty nigger bitch floating in the river," Sammy Black added.

His tone never changed, but his threat spoke a much louder volume.

The phone went dead in Treacherous's ear. He sat on the edge of the bed, mind racing a million miles a minute. What he and Baby had imagined and dreaded had become their reality and worst nightmare. They had kidnapped Baby, and it was killing him. He had no idea what he was going to do. All he knew was that he had to do something. He had figured it was over the money and casino chips they had stolen from the pawnshop. There was no doubt in his mind that if he took the chips and what money they had accumulated to the Irish, both he and Baby would be dead once he gave them what they wanted. Treacherous knew he wasn't equipped or even skilled to go up against the Irish mafia. But the love for another is underestimated until that love is challenged, and that's what Treacherous had in his favor. He loved Baby and her life meant more to him than his own. If the roles were reversed he didn't have to second-guess what Baby would do. He knew the only way he was going to have a fighting chance was if he fought fire with fire. With that being his thought, Treacherous pulled out his 6S and called Ghetto Governor.

Chapter Thirty-six

One hour later . . .

The two Irish henchmen stood guard on opposite sides of the entrance of the abandoned warehouse. They both surveyed their respective areas as best they could from where they stood. Nothing seemed out of the ordinary to either of the men. The darkness made it difficult for them to see but so far. It also posed as a great camouflage for a sneak attack.

The first shot came out of nowhere and slammed into the chest of the Irishman to the far right. He grabbed hold of his upper left chest where the bullet had penetrated his flesh and pierced his heart. His eyes remained wide as he fell to the dirt ground. The other Irishman was busy looking to his left. He never saw or heard the reason why he was now staring down at his sidekick, who lay slumped on the ground.

The Irishman reached for his gun in his shoulder holster. By the time he realized what was happening and drew his weapon it was too late. He was met with the whizzing bullet that had traveled a distance to meet him as soon as he spun back around. The bullet wasted no time introducing itself to the Irishman. It slammed into his skull and split it instantly, like a peeled orange.

The third Irishman sat in the vehicle with his ear buds in listening to classical music. He was oblivious to what was going on outside around him. He never got the chance to react or respond the way his colleagues attempted. Death had already knocked on his door, even before the shattered glass accompanied the bullet that ripped through the side of his head, and covered a great portion of his face.

Treacherous pulled the other silencer-equipped pistol from his waistband. He dipped down low and scaled up alongside of the building. He glanced in each window he cautiously passed by, waving his twin cannons. He stopped at the third window when he noticed a male's back facing him. Treacherous put his hands up to the side of his face and peered into the window. His eyes grew cold. The sight of Baby tied up and bleeding made him see red.

"Muthafucka!" he cursed under his breath.

You could hear the cracking of his knuckles from his now clenched fists. He took a deep breath then sighed. He knew he had to keep calm, for both his and Baby's sakes. He moved farther along the side wall of the building searching for a way in. Like a prayer being answered, Treacherous stumbled across a glassless window at the far end of the building. He peeped in it. He could tell what he was looking at was once an office space. Dust covered a broken desk and a three-legged swivel chair, while damaged empty file cabinets lined the back wall.

He tucked one of his pistols in his waistband then slowly climbed through the window. Once in, he scaled the wall, careful not to step on anything that would make noise or draw any unwanted attention, and he backtracked to where he believed Baby was being held inside the warehouse. He drew his other weapon. He waved them from side to side as he maneuvered his way through the empty spaces, using them as guides.

He heard something up ahead and paused in his tracks. He could hear voices a short distance from where he stood. He began to tiptoe closer to where he had heard the voices coming from. He placed his back flesh against the wall and inched to the edge of it until he reached the panel of the doorless frame. He slowly stretched his neck and peeked around the corner. He nearly lost it at what he saw. It took everything in Treacherous's power not to bum-rush the open room and start blazing. He knew if he did, he'd risk Baby getting caught in the crossfire. He had already told himself the first opportunity he got, the Irishman he had just witnessed assault Baby would be the first to go. Treacherous jumped back. Had he not, the man who had assaulted Baby would have been able to spot him.

Treacherous backpedaled and repositioned himself on the opposite side of the wall out of potential view of either man. From where he stood now, he had a clear view of Baby and the back of the other Irishman. Treacherous scanned the inside of the open room Baby was being held captive in as best he could from where he was.

Think, Treach. He tapped the side of one of his guns up against his head as he weighed his options. As if the gun put it there, an idea popped in his head. Just as he came up with it, the last thing he needed or wanted to hear came out of nowhere and echoed throughout the abandoned warehouse.

Sammy Black looked at his Presidential. "Where's your fucking nigger boyfriend with my money, huh?" Sammy Black grabbed Baby by the back of her head and clenched a fistful of her hair.

Joshua Black stood and watched. He wished it were he who had his hand gripped with Baby's hair. He wanted nothing more than to be the one to kill her.

"He's running out of time," Sammy Black cooed into Baby's ear. He released her hair and pushed her in the back of the head. "I want my fucking money!" he bellowed.

His patience was wearing thin. He stared at Baby. He had witnessed how much she had loved Treacherous by refusing to talk. He didn't know a single woman who could have and would have endured all she had over him, or any other man for that matter. He wondered if Treacherous possessed that same love for her. He hoped that was the case. He believed that would prevent Treacherous from doing anything stupid to avoid any mishaps directed toward Baby. All sorts of thoughts began to invade his mind. But they were put on freeze by the sudden command that slammed into his back and caused him to spin around.

Arthur Love and Andre Randle pulled up near the entrance to the abandoned warehouse. They could see two vehicles up ahead: one in front of the entrance, the other alongside the abandoned building. As they drew near, Arthur Love slammed on brakes.

"Holy shit!" he chimed.

When Andre Randle looked, he could see the lights of the unmarked car beaming down on two bodies slumped in front of the entrance of the warehouse. Arthur Love killed both the lights and the engine.

"You ready for this?" Arthur Love asked.

The two men stared at each other. They both knew that there was a great possibility that either of them may not make it out of this in one piece. But neither of them had any doubt whether they were up for the challenge to see it through.

"Ready as I'll ever be," Andre Randle replied.

"Okay, let's go."

Both men drew their weapons and cautiously exited the vehicle. They covered each other as they moved closer to the building. Andre Randle was the first to reach the back of the car closest to the entrance. He took cover and waved Arthur Love on. He slithered his way toward the side of the driver's door of the vehicle. He jumped back when he saw the Irishman slumped in the front seat with chips of glass poking out of the side of his face and a bullet entry to his dome.

"Clear," he whispered.

Arthur Love scurried over to where Andre Randle stood. He shook his head at the sight of the dead driver. "Freeman," he stated, crediting Treacherous for the handy work.

Andre Randle nodded. "My thoughts exactly."

Once they had secured the perimeter, they scurried into the warehouse one by one with waving guns. Noises could be heard from a distance ahead as soon as they entered the abandoned building. Arthur Love and Andre Randle followed the echo's trail. Randle led the way. The hallway was so dark he nearly tripped over a broken bottle of glass. He was not able to prevent himself from stepping on the glass but was, however, able to lighten the crunching sound it made under his foot. He grimaced and slowly lifted his foot from the broken glass, then sidestepped it and continued moving forward.

Seconds later, he was near the open entrance where all the commotion was taking place. He held up his hand at his partner. He then poked his head inside the open-space room. He did a quick survey. He wasn't surprised to see Sammy Black Jr., but he was surprised not to see Treacherous Freeman. He knew Treacherous was present. It was the only explanation for the dead bodies out front. He figured he had to be hiding somewhere in the immediate area. He did a quick scan of the room for a second time. He tried to see if he could get an inclination where Treacherous may be hiding out. He came up empty-handed. He turned and faced Love. He made hand gestures that indicated he intended to make a move on the count of three. By the time he reached the number three, Love sprang into action.

"Fuck!" Treacherous cursed. *Who the hell are these dumb muthafuckas?* he wondered. They couldn't have shown up at a worse time, he thought. For the past twenty minutes Treacherous had been trying to figure out how to get the drop on the Irishmen without endangering the welfare of Baby. As soon as he had come up with a plan the two unknown men appeared out of nowhere. The crazy thing was they were able to walk straight in. Had Treacherous realized it would have been easier for him to enter through the front versus the back of the enormous warehouse, he would have done just that.

Treacherous eyed the two men carefully. From where he was positioned he could only get a side view of the larger one and barely could see the other man standing a close distance behind him. When the larger man of the two shifted his weapon from Sammy Black to Joshua Black, Treacherous's eyes grew dim.

"No fuckin' way!" he cursed under his breath in disbelief. Treacherous couldn't believe his eyes. He slowly cocked both his weapons.

"Freeze!" Randle yelled as he entered the room. His unexpected presence caught everybody by surprise. Arthur Love entered the room with a sharpshooter's aim, backing Andre Randle up.

All eyes were shifted to the two uninvited guests. Sammy Black shook his head and laughed. He couldn't believe the balls on Arthur Love and Andre Randle.

"You guys don't give up, huh?" Sammy Black joked. He shifted from side to side.

Baby turned to look at the two unidentified men. Her eyes grew cold at the sight of her father and the man who had killed Treacherous's mother.

Arthur Love had his service weapon locked on Joshua Black. He glanced over at Baby. The look on her face caused a sharp pain to jolt through his heart. It was apparent she was not pleased to see him. She shot daggers at him.

Sammy Black noticed the exchange. "Aww!" He sighed in a humorous manner.

"Give me a reason, asshole," Randle snarled.

"No need for all of that," Sammy Black replied in a mocking tone.

"Untie the girl," he ordered. He thought about how uncomfortable it must have been for Arthur Love to see his daughter like that, despite the fact that she was wanted by every law enforcement agency thinkable.

"As you wish." Sammy Black turned toward Baby. He kneeled down and slit the bondage that bound her legs together. He then walked behind her. In one motion, the sharp blade cut the electric chord that bound Baby's hands behind her. Baby's limp body started to swivel to the ground, but Sammy Black caught her in time.

"Fuck you, pig!" he barked as he placed the sharp blade around Baby's neck.

Both Andre Randle and Arthur Love now had their weapons drawn on Sammy Black. "Let her go!" Arthur Love commanded.

Sammy Black responded with a sinister laugh. A sudden detection of movement drew his attention in front of him. Out of reflex, Sammy reacted and opened Pandora's box. A painful cry filled the air as an array of bullets accompanied it.

Treacherous had watched Baby's father and the man who had killed his mother as they tried to negotiate with Sammy Black. He was surprised when he saw Sammy releasing Baby. He knew overall he had the advantage. No one could see him but from where he stood he could see all of them. Sammy Black was who he mostly had in his range. He had a clear view of him and intended to take full advantage. His initial plan was foiled when Sammy Black snatched Baby up and placed the knife around her neck. Treacherous tightened his grip around his pistols. Sammy Black rocked back and forth from side to side. Treacherous followed his every move with his weapons. The way Sammy Black had Baby yoked up, it was difficult for Treacherous to get a clear shot.

He grimaced in frustration. He knew he had to come up with another plan and fast. He did a quick survey of the room, contemplating his next move. Before he could come up with another plan, the sudden movement in front of Sammy Black Jr. and Andre Randle triggered off a chain reaction. Treacherous watched as pandemonium broke loose. Seeing the way Baby was being handled infuriated Treacherous. That was all the motivation he needed. He barged in the open room and joined the festivities.

The black cat's body somersaulted in the air from the bullet that ripped through its pregnant belly, ending what lives she had left of her nine. She had chosen the wrong time to use her last life to stroll through the open space. Sammy Black's shot inspired Arthur Love and Andre Randle to take cover, but not before Andre Randle delivered a shot of his own in Sammy Black and Baby's direction. He and Arthur Love both mistook Sammy Black's shot as an act of aggression and immediately went into battle mode.

Sammy Black yanked Baby by the neck. He used her as a shield. Fortunately for them, the bullet Andre Randle let off veered to the left before it reached them. A relieved Sammy pulled Baby closer to him. He tossed his blade to the ground and drew his gun, which was now pressed up against Baby's temple. The way he was positioned had him secured and shielded from Arthur Love and Andre Randle. He had no clue that his position made him an open target behind him though. The distress in his cousin's voice was the notification he received informing him that imminent danger was near. Sammy Black spun around. Had he not looked first, he may have made a huge mistake. He pushed Baby toward the two detectives and braced himself. He was met with a bear hug that sent him stumbling backward. He didn't realize the real reason why he stumbled until it was too late.

Joshua Black tackled his cousin onto the ground. His decision prevented the two shots Treacherous let off, intended for Sammy Black's head, from reaching their final destination. He was, however, unsuccessful with stopping the next two shots that rang out. He shielded Sammy Black as best he could. He watched as the bullet tore through Sammy Black's throat. He returned three shots of his own, intended for Treacherous, from his 9 mm right before he was caught by surprise.

The second bullet from one of Treacherous's cannons slammed into Joshua Black's chest. The impact sent him crashing to the ground. It also threw his aim off, causing the shots he had fired to scatter. One came close to a ducking Treacherous's head; another ricocheted off a steel beam and kicked back in his direction. The third shot curved in the direction where Baby stood frozen, and it coincidentally grazed her across her midsection. He noticed that both Sammy and Joshua Black were down and no longer factors.

Treacherous spit three more shots in Arthur Love and Andre Randle's direction as a diversion. Baby's screams drew his attention to her. He saw her belly over and stumble off to the side. Her cries fueled his actions. His only thought was of reaching her.

Arthur Love and Andre Randle witnessed the shootout from a safe distance. Neither man knew what to do. It wasn't until Arthur Love saw his daughter get struck by a stray bullet that he reacted. He came out of hiding. His visibility triggered off a barrage of bullets thrown in his direction. Arthur Love ducked and took cover behind a metal barrel. He let off two shots in the direction from which the bullets had come. He cautiously raised his head up over the barrel. The first thing he noticed was Baby removing a gun from Sammy Black's lifeless body. He knew he couldn't let her gain possession of a weapon. The scene seemed to be déjà vu and he knew he couldn't let that happen. Without giving it a second thought, Arthur Love rose up, fully erect. He pumped four shots to his left and scurried toward his right simultaneously over to where Baby was located. Surprisingly there were no shots returned.

Baby had just pried Sammy Black's pistol from his hand. She tripped over her own feet trying to run for cover. She had peeped what her father was trying to do. She knew exactly how smart he was. After all, he had taught her everything she knew. She turned into the nearest doorless room.

Arthur Love speedily loaded his weapon and took flight after her. The room was just as huge as the one they were just in. A short distance ahead he saw Baby approaching the next doorway. From where he stood, he had a clear shot of her. He grimaced. Rather than putting her down like he knew he should, he let off a warning shot. "It's all over, Baby," he called out.

Baby heard the explosion of her father's warning shot. She cursed and sucked her teeth. She abruptly stopped in her tracks. She had a feeling that if she kept running her father would surely shoot her. She didn't want to take that chance. She turned to face Arthur Love with a murderous look plastered across her face. She scowled at the sight of his gun. The last time the two of them were in the situation they were faced with now, it didn't end well, thought Baby. She didn't think today would be any different.

She stared at the man she once loved with all of her being for a moment. She barely recognized him. He may have looked like her father to her, but he was not the man she knew. The man before her was just a police officer doing his job. Baby felt nothing for Arthur Love. She realized the little bit of love she once possessed for him had faded. But Baby knew Arthur Love still loved her. She could see it in his eyes. She preyed on her father's weakness and cocked her weapon.

Arthur Love stood locked with his weapon on Baby. He had a bad feeling about the Mexican standoff he was faced with between him and his daughter. His worst thought became a reality once again. Something told him that, just like before, Baby was not going to back down. His suspicion was confirmed when Baby pulled the hammer back on her first weapon.

Arthur Love raised his weapon higher. "Please, Baby!" he pleaded. "Don't make me do this."

Arthur Love could not believe he was back in the predicament he was in. It was as if it was déjà vu all over again. He had played the last scenario over a hundred times in his head. He'd wondered if he had the chance would he do anything different than he had that eventful night. He knew it was one thing to say you would do the right thing, but it was another thing when the right thing cost you something or someone you loved. The last time, he had let Baby and her boyfriend get away, after she had killed her mother, his wife, in front of him. He allowed his paternal feelings to get the best of him when he knew he should have been doing his job by upholding the law, daughter or not. More effort could have been put into demanding she surrender to him. The marksman he was, he knew he could have ended Baby's life with one shot rather than grazing her. There were lot of should haves, could haves, and would haves, he thought. The question was how would he handle the situation now? Only he knew the answer to that.

Baby could tell he was fighting with his emotions based on the twisted and distorted facial expressions he made while eyeing her down. She felt no remorse. "Do what you gotta do, Detective," Baby retorted, addressing him by his rank. She knew it would sting.

Her father grimaced. "Don't tempt me, goddamit!" he boomed.

"Don't tempt me. Muthafucka!" she returned. Her gun was now level with her father's heart.

"Baby, put the gun down or—"

"Or what?" she barked. Tears were now streaming down her face. They were not tears of sorrow but rather of anger. Hatred and resentment swept through her entire body. All of the pain and anger inside of Baby came to a head and was released. Without thought, Baby squeezed the trigger of her gun. She never got to see whether the shot landed.

Arthur Love saw the bullet headed in his direction. He had even seen it before Baby had delivered it. He could see it in her eyes before she had pulled the trigger, that she had reached the point of no return. When their eyes first met and he noticed the murderous look in his daughter's, he knew he had to prepare himself to take her down if she carried through with what he believed to be her thoughts. His instincts went into survival mode. He saw murder in Baby's eyes and knew he was the intended victim. Arthur Love attempted to squeeze the trigger of his own weapon, but something happened. Something just made him stop. He accepted what was taking place. He just couldn't bring himself to kill his own daughter. Instead, he sacrificed his own life.

The bullet plunged into Arthur Love's lower abdomen, just below his bulletproof vest. His weapon dropped to the ground. He grabbed hold of his stomach and bellied over. His semi-limp body pummeled the ground. He fought to breathe as blood invaded his breathing passage. The room seemed to be spinning. Arthur Love let out a disgusting-sounding cough. He rolled over to his side in an attempt to minimize the flow of blood that was trickling down his throat. He took short breaths to preserve what little oxygen he had left in him. With each breath, Arthur Love felt himself growing weaker and weaker. His entire life flashed before his eyes as he lay on his side dying. He stared into the distance.

What strength he had remaining he used to focus on the image a few feet in front of him. Arthur Love grimaced. A tear rolled out of the side of his right eye. His eyes locked with Baby's for a second time as she lay on the ground bleeding. He'd never know what happened to her. That would be his final thought, before death stood over him and took what little life he had left inside his body.

Andre Randle came out from where he was hiding as soon as Arthur Love made his move. He backed his partner up, waving his gun from top to bottom and side to side in the open space while Arthur Love took chase after his daughter. Andre Randle was surprised that no shots were fired in retaliation to Arthur Love's shots. He remembered the direction from which the first set of shots had come. He was sure the shooter had to have been Treacherous.

He moved stealth-like through the open room in the particular direction. Reflexively he jumped back when he saw an image of who he believed to be Treacherous bolting from one room to the next. He waited until the image had disappeared before he followed suit. He knew that was the direction Arthur Love and Baby had gone in. He put a pep in his step. Instead of going through the doorless frame he had seen Treacherous dip through, Andre Randle detoured and walked up farther to the next doorway.

He popped his head in. Once he saw the coast was clear, he entered the room. He crossed one foot over the other as he moved forward, snail-like. As he had hoped, he noticed that there was another doorless frame ahead that seemed to put him on the other side of the room behind him that Treacherous had ducked into. The thunderous roar of a gunshot made him jerk and stop in his tracks. He listened to the echo of the shot and followed its trail. A few feet ahead, he could hear voices. When he finally reached the doorway of the room, he had no time to think. He only had a split second to make a decision.

Blood flew out of Joshua Black's mouth as he regained consciousness. He struggled to sit up. He grabbed hold of his shirt and ripped it open. His dress shirt buttons wildly popped off, one by one.

"Thanks, ol' chum." Joshua Black tapped on the Kevlar vest that had saved his life on countless occasions. He blinked until his vision became clear. He looked over to his left and grimaced.

Sammy Black's lifeless eyes stared back at him. His bullet-riddled body sat upright against the wall. Joshua Black had lain helplessly and watched as the black detective pumped his cousin full of lead. The last thing he remembered from before he blacked out was the same detective pursuing the boyfriend of the girl he had grown to hate.

"The Lord giveth and the Lord taketh." Joshua Black said a quick final prayer for his cousin, then stood up and started heading in the opposite direction from which he saw Andre Randle and Treacherous go. He thought it best to regroup. His uncle's death had already gone unavenged. The last thing he wanted to see was his cousin's death end the same way. Once outside, he scurried over to the nearest vehicle. He removed the dead chauffeur from the driver's seat of his cousin's car and hopped in. He wiped the blood and brain matter as best he could with his hand off the front window, then snatched the gear shift into reverse.

Treacherous's eyes shot open. He had just regained consciousness after hitting his head on the side of the steel beam. He could feel the side of his head. A knot had already formed and he felt a little discombobulated. He'd rather have a slight concussion of some sort and a knot on his head than be lifeless. He had dived out of the line of fire of Arthur Love's shots just in time, but lost his balance and fell. Luckily, he saw the direction in which Baby had run and was sure her father had gone in pursuit.

He retrieved the gun that dropped out of his hand when he took cover. He tucked it in his waistband then reached for the sawed-off double-barrel pump he had in the duffle strapped to his back. A shot rang out in the air. Treacherous realized the shot had come from the direction in which Baby had run. He took flight, navigating his way through the open rooms. He was already familiar with the maze structure from when he had first entered the abandoned warehouse. In no time, he stood in front of the doorless frame of the room Baby and Arthur Love were in. Treacherous had arrived just in time to witness the standoff between his lady and her father. He was, however, too late to prevent either of them from pulling the trigger. He watched as Arthur Love fell backward but when he saw Baby doing the same, and falling to the ground, he lost it. A mixture of confusion and anger filled his body. He knew there was no way her father could have shot her. Treacherous looked to the left of him, where the shot had come from. His eyes dimmed low, nostrils flared up, and jaws tightened as he rushed into the room.

"Motherfucka!" he barked as he let loose the double barrels in Andre Randle's direction.

The buckshot tore into Andre Randle's chest and knocked him back out of the room and through the doorway. Convinced he couldn't have survived the shot, Treacherous put the double-barrel shotgun back in the duffle then drew the gun in his waistband. He couldn't believe after all of these years he had just managed to kill the man who was responsible for his mother's death. It was not how he had imagined it, but dead was dead, he concluded. His attention was actually focused on someone else. He wanted nothing more than to stand over Andre Randle's lifeless body and remind him of the words he had said to him the day he had killed his mother. But the remaining bullets he had in his pistol were reserved. Treacherous took a second glance back before he made a beeline a few feet ahead. He was now standing over Baby's father.

Arthur Love looked up at him with pleading eyes. Treacherous could tell he wanted to say something, but he did not grant him a dying man's last words. Instead, he pointed one of his guns down at Arthur Love and pulled the trigger continuously. He released the remaining four bullets from one of his weapons. Two slammed into Arthur Love's face in rapid succession. The other two ripped into his chest. Had there been more bullets in the gun he would have fed them all to Arthur Love. The clicking sound indicating the gun was empty brought

Treacherous back from his temporary zone. He rushed over to where Baby lay.

"Baby!" he called out. He dropped to the ground and snatched up her body. He brushed her hair out of her face and wiped the blood from her mouth.

"Baby?" he repeated.

This time he shook her. He held her head in his arms. He leaned down and pressed his ear up against her heart. He heard nothing. He squeezed her wrist to check her pulse. Again, he felt nothing. He tapped Baby on the face. "Babe? Wake up!" The pain could be heard in his pleads.

Treacherous's upper lip began to quiver. Water filled his eyes until they couldn't hold it any longer. He tapped her again, only this time harder. "Baby, get the fuck up!" he cursed. A nervous feeling began to sweep through his body. Treacherous looked around. For the first time since everything had jumped off, he was afraid. Not afraid of getting caught, but afraid of being alone. Baby was all he had. Without her he had nothing, he believed.

His mind traveled back to the stories he had read about his parents and their demise, and he couldn't help but see the irony in what he was faced with now. He remembered how he had read about how his own father thought he had lost his mother and held court in the middle of the highway and how she had tried to take her own life until she had found out she was carrying him inside of her. The thought of his legendary parents had Treacherous comparing his and Baby's own reign of terror to theirs. He thought back to how Baby was in awe when he told her the story about the pact his parents had made with each other to end their own life if something happened to the other, and how his birth had delayed his mother's death. He reflected on how she had admired the tale and had said she had wanted that same type of love between them.

All sorts of thoughts flashed through Treacherous's mind, mostly images of Baby. The first time they had made love appeared in his thoughts, followed by a scene of Baby dancing in Club Aqua. Treacherous squeezed his eyes tightly. That caused a flood of tears to burst out of them. The salty tears stained his face and managed to slip into his mouth. He shook uncontrollably. He rocked back and forth with Baby held tight in his arms. The last image that played in his mind was of Baby's smile. She stood there in a beam of light gesturing for Treacherous to come to her. Treacherous fought with the decision that seemed to take control over his thoughts.

What's the point? he questioned. He searched for answers within himself. He knew if the shoe were on the other foot, Baby would not have hesitated to make the decision he struggled with. He looked down and stared at her for a moment, admiring her beauty.

This is not how it's supposed to end, he said to himself. He wiped the tears from his eyes, then lowered his head. He gently pressed his lips up against Baby's and kissed them. He noticed they were still warm. He didn't want to remove his lips from hers but knew he had to. It was just a matter of time before the place was crawling with police. At that moment, he felt there was no other reason to live.

Treacherous took a deep breath, then closed his eyes. He pulled the shotgun out of the duffle, then looked down at Baby and sighed. "See you soon," he then said right before he put the gun to his temple. He curled his finger around the trigger and applied a little pressure. He knew he was stalling and the thoughts racing through his mind made it no better. Images of his mother, Baby, and what he believed his father looked like flashed through his mind as he pressed the barrel tight against his dome. It was low, but it was effective. Just as Treacherous was about to pull the trigger, he heard a noise. No matter how low it was, he knew where the sound had come from. It was a whisper he was all too familiar with. The word *no* echoed throughout his ears and traveled through his soul warming his heart.

He lowered the gun from his head and peered down. He was met with a partial smile and misty eyes as Baby stared up at him. Her sudden resurrection breathed new life back into him. He was at a loss for words. He knew there was no time for talking though. Time was of the essence and he didn't have any to waste. The last time they had found themselves in a heated gun battle, it was she who had to get them to safety and get him help. Now the shoe was on the other foot. It was now Treacherous's turn to get them out of dodge and get Baby some medical attention.

Treacherous tossed the shotgun back in the duffle, then scooped Baby up. Minutes later, he had her laid out in the back seat of the car.

"Don't worry, bae. I got you," he turned around and directed to Baby. Although she had closed her eyes again, he knew she could hear him. "Once again, we gonna make it up outta this shit, like we always do. Or die trying!" he ended.

He waited to see if she would respond or acknowledge him. She didn't open her eyes, but her lips moved until a smile was able to break through. That's all he needed. Treacherous turned back around and threw the car into drive.

Epilogue

The sound of a squeaky door caused him to jump out of his sleep and his eyes to shoot open. When the door flung open, he saw an image appear in the doorway. The bright light behind it made it difficult for him to make out who it was. But when the figure emerged he was surprised to see his friend standing in the middle of his hospital room, alive and well. If he were able to smile he would have.

"I thought I had nine lives," were the first words Andre Randle spoke as soon as he entered Arthur Love's room. He had been coming in and checking on him for the past week. He had finally caught him awake. He shook his head at his friend's present condition. Love's jaw was wired and he had a brace around his neck. As badly as he wanted to, Randle knew, he couldn't respond or laugh at his remarks. Although it was funny, Randle couldn't have been any closer to the truth. When Arthur Love woke up in the hospital, it was the first thing he had thought.

"That means we're two lucky cats," Randle continued with his pun. He was now sitting next to Love's bedside. "Had it not been for my Kevlar, it may be a different story though," he added, referring to the bulletproof vest that had saved his life. He too had a close call back at the warehouse when Treacherous pumped what was intended to be his chest with buckshot.

Love blinked his eyes as a means to agree with Randle. He had seen when Treacherous had spun around and let off the shotgun in Randle's direction as he lay on the ground fighting for his own life. He was sure Randle was a dead man, which was why he was both surprised and glad to see him when he first entered the room. He listened as Randle continued.

"You know what else that means." It was more of a statement than a question. "It means we get one more shot at apprehending your daughter and Freeman." He let his words marinate.

Arthur Love's eyes widened, flickered, and then closed to imagine that day.

"My thoughts exactly, partner." Randle nodded as he patted Love's right hand.

To be continued . . .

Ride or Die Chick 5

ORDER FORM
URBAN BOOKS, LLC
97 N. 18th Street
Wyandanch, NY 11798

Name (please print):_____

Address: _____

City/State: _____

Zip: _____

QTY	TITLES	PRICE

Shipping and handling-add $3.50 for 1st book, then $1.75 for each additional book.

Please send a check payable to:

Urban Books, LLC

Please allow 4–6 weeks for delivery

ORDER FORM
URBAN BOOKS, LLC
97 N. 18th Street
Wyandanch, NY 11798

Name:(please print):_____

Address: _____

City/State: _____

Zip: _____

QTY	TITLES	PRICE
	16 On The Block	$14.95
	A Girl From Flint	$14.95
	A Pimp's Life	$14.95
	Baltimore Chronicles	$14.95
	Baltimore Chronicles 2	$14.95
	Betrayal	$14.95
	Black Diamond	$14.95
	Black Diamond 2	$14.95
	Black Friday	$14.95
	Both Sides Of The Fence	$14.95
	Both Sides Of The Fence 2	$14.95
	California Connection	$14.95

Shipping and handling-add $3.50 for 1st book, then $1.75 for each additional book.
Please send a check payable to:
Urban Books, LLC
Please allow 4–6 weeks for delivery

ORDER FORM
URBAN BOOKS, LLC
97 N. 18th Street
Wyandanch, NY 11798

Name (please print):_____

Address: _____

City/State: _____

Zip: _____

QTY	TITLES	PRICE
	California Connection 2	$14.95
	Cheesecake And Teardrops	$14.95
	Congratulations	$14.95
	Crazy In Love	$14.95
	Cyber Case	$14.95
	Denim Diaries	$14.95
	Diary Of A Mad First Lady	$14.95
	Diary Of A Stalker	$14.95
	Diary Of A Street Diva	$14.95
	Diary Of A Young Girl	$14.95
	Dirty Money	$14.95
	Dirty To The Grave	$14.95

Shipping and handling-add $3.50 for 1st book, then $1.75 for each additional book.
Please send a check payable to:
      Urban Books, LLC
Please allow 4-6 weeks for delivery

ORDER FORM
URBAN BOOKS, LLC
97 N. 18th Street
Wyandanch, NY 11798

Name (please print):_____

Address: _____

City/State: _____

Zip: _____

QTY	TITLES	PRICE
	Gunz And Roses	$14.95
	Happily Ever Now	$14.95
	Hell Has No Fury	$14.95
	Hush	$14.95
	If It Isn't love	$14.95
	Kiss Kiss Bang Bang	$14.95
	Last Breath	$14.95
	Little Black Girl Lost	$14.95
	Little Black Girl Lost 2	$14.95
	Little Black Girl Lost 3	$14.95
	Little Black Girl Lost 4	$14.95
	Little Black Girl Lost 5	$14.95

Shipping and handling-add $3.50 for 1st book, then $1.75 for each additional book.
Please send a check payable to:
    Urban Books, LLC
Please allow 4-6 weeks for delivery